THE CURSED SCARAB

Don't miss an adventure at the Haunted Museum!

THE HAUNTED MUSEUM

THE CURSED SCARAB

BOOK FOUR

Suzanne Weyn

SCHOLASTIC INC.

Copyright © 2015 by Suzanne Weyn

All rights reserved. Published by Scholastic Inc., *Publishers since 1920*. SCHOLASTIC and associated logos are trademarks and/or registered trademarks of Scholastic Inc.

ISBN 978-0-545-58849-2

12 11 10 9 8 7 6 5 4 3 2 1   15 16 17 18 19 20/0

Printed in the U.S.A.   40
First printing, May 2015

The text type was set in Old Style 7.
Book design by Abby Kuperstock

For lovers of the creepy, strange, and mystifying.

THE CURSED SCARAB

INTRODUCTION

Welcome. You have arrived at the Haunted Museum. It's a place where dreams are made — bad dreams! Ghostly phantasms float by. When you least expect it, a hand grabs your throat. An old music box plays a tune you'd rather forget. A painting you are viewing is also viewing you.

I opened the Haunted Museum many, *many* years ago. And I've been adding to its special displays for longer than I can recall.

Some say the museum has become a worldwide chain — just an entertaining fraud for the amusement of tourists.

Others see something more mysterious, more sinister within its walls.

Either way, no one escapes unaffected by what they find within the museum. The items that touch your hands will come back to touch your life in a most terrifying manner.

Take, for instance, the case of Taylor Mason, who has always wondered what it would be like to be an ancient Egyptian princess. But she needs to be careful what she wishes for. When she comes into possession of an ancient artifact, she unleashes a terrifying evil into the world.

Happy Haunting,

Belladonna Bloodstone

Founder and Head Curator

THE HAUNTED MUSEUM

I DON'T KNOW how a cheesy place like the Haunted Museum ever got hold of such valuable treasures," Taylor Mason's father griped as they stood in line outside the Haunted Museum. "I can't believe we have to come *here* to see them."

"What's wrong with here?" Taylor asked. She didn't share her dad's dismay. This was her first time at the Haunted Museum and she was thrilled to be there. She looked ahead at the banner outside the large brick building and smiled. NEW DISCOV-ERY! THE LOST TREASURES OF NEFERTITI!

"These artifacts should be at a real museum with proper security," her father said, his voice taking on that familiar tone he used when he began a lecture. Professor Mason taught classes on ancient Egypt at the nearby university. The Masons' home was full of books about ancient Egypt, many of them written by him. Any surface that wasn't a bookshelf held Egyptian artifacts or models of famous sites or landmarks.

Mrs. Mason, Taylor's mom, was also inter-ested in the history of Egypt. She had written a play about Queen Nefertiti, wife of the pharaoh Akhenaten. A local theater group had even done a performance of it. The county newspaper had given it a great review, calling the play "a thrilling look into a lost world."

The fact that ancient Egypt was a huge part of the Mason family's life was fine by Taylor. She thought it was all extremely interesting, from the beautiful art to the incredible buildings, and wished she could have lived in the times of the pharaohs. Sometimes she daydreamed about being an ancient Egyptian princess.

Taylor even blew her dark hair straight and wore it in a blunt cut to her chin, in the style of ancient Egypt. If she was feeling brave, she'd tie a thin gold cord across her long bangs and wear white to really highlight the Egyptian look.

Some kids in school made fun of her for dressing up when it wasn't Halloween, but her good friends called her Queen Cleo, after the ancient Queen Cleopatra, even when she wore jeans and a plain T-shirt. They understood it was a look that came out of her true interest in Egyptian culture and not just a show, so they thought it was cool.

But today, since seventh grade had just ended for summer vacation, Taylor was free to attend the exhibit as soon as it opened. Unfortunately, it seemed like a lot of people had the same idea, and she and her dad stood in a long line of families and groups of teenagers.

A tall boy with a blond crew cut stood in front of Taylor in line. He had on a black T-shirt covered with the symbols of ancient Egyptian writing. Hieroglyphics.

As they moved forward, Taylor was so busy looking at the symbols, trying to figure out what each one meant, that she accidently stepped on the back of his sneaker. The boy whirled to face her. Behind his black-framed glasses, his eyes were a piercing blue.

"Sorry," Taylor murmured, embarrassed.

He didn't seem angry but he wasn't smiling, either. "Nice haircut," he said. "Very Egyptian."

Taylor squinted at him, uncertain. Was he making fun of her? "Thanks," Taylor said cautiously. "I like your T-shirt."

The boy held out the hem to gaze down at it. "It spells my name — Jason — in hieroglyphics."

"That's cool," Taylor said. "Where did you find it?"

"Online," he replied. "I'm always browsing the ancient Egypt sites. I'm kind of an expert on it."

"Really," Taylor said, more as a comment than a question. He certainly seemed to think a lot of himself. Jason smiled a tiny bit and nodded, then turned back around.

"You've made a new friend," Professor Mason remarked.

Taylor scowled at her father. Jason had ears — he could hear! "Dad, shhhh!" she whispered.

"Sorry," her father said more quietly.

Jason was *not* a new friend! She barely knew him. Besides that, Taylor didn't even particularly like his self-impressed manner. Kind of an expert! Really?!

"Hey, look at that photo." Professor Mason pointed to the doorway. "Isn't she something?"

The banner by the main entrance featured a picture of the famous head and shoulders statue of Queen Nefertiti carved by the ancient Egyptian sculptor Thutmose. The bust showed her adorned by the well-known conelike crown. The heavy-lidded, dark, almond-shaped eyes were rimmed in black kohl. Her long neck stretched forward regally, drawing the viewer's eye to the many levels of her wide necklace of semiprecious stones.

From reading about the royal queen, Taylor knew that the name Nefertiti meant "the beautiful one has come." To Taylor she was more than lovely. Everything about Nefertiti was magical and glamorous. The queen embodied all that was intriguing and mysterious about ancient Egypt. Taylor could hardly believe that soon she would be viewing objects that the intriguing queen had actually touched with her own hands.

As the line moved forward, Taylor noticed security guards in identical black pants, white shirts, and black sport jackets stationed all around the sidewalk outside the building. Stone-faced behind the mirrored lenses of their sunglasses, they balanced on the balls of their feet, pivoting this way and that.

"There are security guards here," Taylor told her dad, recalling his concerns about the artifacts. "Lots of them."

He scanned the area and nodded. "Well, that's good, at least."

"How valuable *is* this stuff, anyway?" Taylor asked her father.

"A treasure thought to be lost to the world, newly discovered, and of the size I've heard it described?" Professor Mason said. "Any of the pieces would be priceless, just for having been among the treasure of Akhenaten and Nefertiti."

Taylor was even more impatient to see the collection, but the line didn't seem to be moving at all.

"Will you be all right here for a moment?" her dad asked, nodding toward the restroom.

"Sure," Taylor said, "but if this line moves and you're not back, I'm going to see the treasure without you!"

As her father walked away, Jason turned back to Taylor. "You know, the value of the treasure isn't why it's here at the Haunted Museum."

"Oh? Why, then?" Taylor asked.

Jason looked at her with a grin. "Because it's *haunted*!"

"Oh sure!" Taylor said. "Totally haunted." She knew they were at the Haunted Museum, but she'd never believed in the supernatural. She was just there to see Nefertiti's treasure.

"It's more like *cursed* than haunted," Jason went on.

"Every other treasure found in Egypt is 'cursed,'" Taylor said.

"Yeah, but this one in particular," Jason said. "Smenkhkare was this wizard sort of guy, and he ruled with Akhenaten toward the end of his reign. Nefertiti's treasure was stolen and Smenkhkare put a curse on whoever stole it."

"Did Smenkhkare's curse work?" Taylor asked.

Jason shrugged. "Probably. All I know is what they said on the Haunted Museum website. That the treasures of Nefertiti are among the most mysterious and strange Egyptian collections ever uncovered."

"That assumes you believe in ancient curses at all," Professor Mason said, stepping back into his place in line next to Taylor.

"Of course not," Taylor said. She knew it was superstition, and it wasn't like her dad had been cursed in all his years in the field.

"I totally believe in ancient curses," Jason replied with conviction. "It's been proven. They're real."

2

THE LINE began moving and soon they were in the front lobby of the Haunted Museum. It was dark with swirling smoke. Jason turned back to Taylor. "Don't worry. It's just dry ice," he said.

Taylor rolled her eyes and nodded. Of course it was! It annoyed her that he thought she was so dumb.

"This place is kind of lame," Taylor murmured to her father as an electronic skeleton dressed to be the pirate Long John Silver rose from its coffin and shook its sword at passersby.

"It is," her father agreed. "I don't know how a tourist trap ever acquired these treasures. Let's just see them and go."

They came to a sign with an arrow that read: THIS WAY TO THE THREE-HEADED COW. "Aww, can't we at least see the cow before we leave?" Taylor asked with a big fake grin.

Her father chuckled. "Let's focus on the Lost Treasures for now," he said. "They've been hidden away for thousands of years, and I'm dying to see them."

Finally, they came to a long, beautifully lit room full of glass cases, where the treasures were displayed. Two mummies stood in their sarcophagi against the far wall. A larger-than-life poster depicting Nefertiti hung over some writing. Taylor and Professor Mason went over to read it. Jason tagged along with them as though he was now part of their group, and Taylor wasn't sure whether she wanted to keep talking to him or for him to go away.

Together they read the information about how Nefertiti's husband, the pharaoh Akhenaten, had done away with the old Egyptian gods: Horus, Anubis, Isis, etc. He'd started a new religion that worshipped Aten, the sun.

Some Egyptians took to the new sun worship. But others were angered by it and wanted the old ways back. Some of them believed that the source of all Akhenaten and Nefertiti's power was contained in the treasure they kept locked away in one of their temples; if they could take or destroy the treasure, the rulers would fall from power and the old gods would return. One night the temple was broken into and all the most valuable treasure was stolen. Only now, thousands of years later, had the treasure been uncovered, hidden deep in Egypt in a bat-filled cave.

"Why would the Egyptian government ever let this treasure be displayed here so fast?" Professor Mason asked in amazement. "It doesn't look as if there's been time to evaluate or even catalog the find."

"Belladonna Bloodstone has many friends around the world." Turning toward the person who had just spoken, Taylor observed a petite woman who gave off a powerful energy. Her raven hair was pulled back tightly in a twist that high-lighted a face of sharp angles. Her dark eyes sparkled. She was dressed in a black suit, and her arms jangled with many silver bangles.

"Are you Belladonna Bloodstone?" Taylor guessed.

"The owner of the Haunted Museum?" Jason added.

"I am," she replied with an accent Taylor couldn't identify.

"How did you ever get ahold of these priceless treasures?" Professor Mason inquired.

Belladonna Bloodstone grinned. "The head curator of the Museum of Egyptian Antiquities in Cairo, Egypt, a man named Dr. Bey, is a friend of mine. I took care of a little matter for him once, and he owed me a favor."

"Well, this is some favor!" Professor Mason marveled.

Belladonna Bloodstone smiled mysteriously. "The treasure will be returned to Egypt after a month, and is now under the utmost security, I assure you," she said, nodding toward the guards. "Enjoy yourselves, but be very careful to do as the signs say."

"What signs?" Jason asked.

Belladonna Bloodstone laughed. "What signs?!

You mean you haven't noticed them?" she asked. She spread her arms to indicate the walls around them. Signs that read DO NOT TOUCH hung everywhere.

"Oh, but of course," Professor Mason said. "No daughter of mine would try to handle antiquities without proper training."

"Good. It's very important. No matter what happens, do not touch anything." Smiling, Belladonna Bloodstone backed up and disappeared into the crowd viewing the treasures.

Taylor and Jason walked together ahead of Professor Mason as they made their way through the exhibit. Both of them were so fascinated by the objects that they hardly spoke. Beside the gold and stone pieces, there were jewel-encrusted statues carved from ebony. Taylor especially liked a statue of a big-eared, short-coated cat with emerald eyes.

Taylor leaned close when she noticed a large round object. The shape of a big insect was carved into the blue stone. Taylor knew that it was a scarab, a common image in Egyptian art.

"They really loved the dung beetle," Jason commented.

"A what kind of beetle?" Taylor asked. She'd never really thought about it before.

"Yeah. A dung beetle," Jason confirmed. "Since these guys worshipped Aten, the sun god, they liked the round dung balls the beetles rolled up. The beetles laid their eggs in the dung balls."

"Ew!" Taylor said, wrinkling her nose. She leaned in closer to the case. "Now I see it," she said. "Those marks are the wings, all folded up close to the body. And there's the head and the pincers at the top."

"Exactly," Jason said in that superior, smug way that was really starting to annoy her.

"This one is much larger than the scarabs I've seen," she said as Jason bent close beside her.

"Stop!" someone shouted.

Taylor lifted her head quickly at the sound of the voice. At first she thought she and Jason were being scolded for leaning so close to the case.

But then she saw what was really happening.

A guard was struggling with a man dressed all in black. His eyes were shaded with dark sunglasses and a knit cap covered his head. He flailed his arms and writhed in the guard's grip.

Other members of the security team approached to help but as they neared the thief, he broke free and ran.

Another guard tackled the robber, and the two of them tumbled backward into the glass case holding the scarab.

Taylor and Jason leaped backward as the case overturned, smashing to the ground. Shards of glass scattered everywhere and the case's contents slid in all directions.

Alarms blared. Museum visitors hurried away, frightened.

The man in black crawled free from under the guard to lunge for the blue scarab beside Taylor's foot.

On impulse, Taylor snapped up the scarab before he could get it.

In the next second, three guards piled onto the man, pinning him to the floor.

"Stand back everyone!" cried a man who seemed to be in charge of security. "We've been waiting for you to show up, Valdry," he said, stooping to talk to the man on the floor.

"I've done nothing. You can't hold me," the man shouted angrily, his voice revealing a French accent.

"Done nothing?!" the head guard scoffed. He snatched the dark glasses from Valdry's face.

Valdry cringed and shielded his eyes. "I have an eye condition. I must have my glasses."

"You call this nothing!" the guard asked as he handed the sunglasses back to Valdry. "You tried to take this scarab from the archaeologists who uncovered it back in Egypt. When that failed you came here to try to steal it. We've been watching you for weeks."

As the guards pulled Valdry to his feet, Taylor gazed at the blue scarab she held. Only then did she realize it vibrated, and the sensation was becoming stronger with every passing second. The tingle ran up her arm and traveled into her shoulder, up her neck, and into the back of her skull.

What was happening? The room was swirling . . . and then the Haunted Museum, and everyone and everything around Taylor, melted away.

3

Taylor stood at the opening of a cave, looking out onto a rolling, dune-filled desert. Narrowing her eyes into slits to block the blinding sun, Taylor felt strangely at home in this place.

She realized that she still held the scarab, and lifted it so that the round blue beetle appeared to blot out the sun's yellow, glowing disc. When viewed in that way, the scarab was exactly the size of the sun in the sky.

Squinting up at the burning yellow orb, she felt the scarab grow warmer in her hand. A tingling sensation emanated from the blue stone. It ran up her arm until the pins-and-needles feeling engulfed her limb. Part of her wanted to drop the scarab, to make the strange feeling go away. Yet somehow she knew not to do that.

Her mission was too urgent for her to give up now.

How did she know? Taylor wasn't sure. There seemed to be two people alive in her body. There was Taylor, who didn't understand what was happening — and someone else was present as well. The other person had been in this desert many times and knew full well what she needed to do.

"Aten," she said, in a commanding voice not entirely her own. "Pour your power into this scarab named Khepri so that I might possess the might of the universe in my very hand."

The scarab in Taylor's hand glowed with a vivid yellow light. A high-pitched ringing made Taylor cringe until she couldn't stand it any longer, and she fainted to the sandy ground.

. . .

"Drop it inside, please, miss."

Taylor blinked slowly at the guard who had first tackled Valdry. She held a wooden case out for Taylor to deposit the scarab into. What had happened? Where had the desert gone?

"Oh," Taylor gasped, returning to reality. "Sure," she said, setting the scarab into the case.

"How about thanking her for saving it?" Taylor's father told the guard as he came to stand beside his daughter. "That was pretty fast thinking, wouldn't you say?"

"We were on the job," the guard said. "The scarab was never really in danger."

Professor Mason shook his head and hugged Taylor close. "Are you all right?" he asked.

"I got cut on some glass from the case," Jason said, as though the question had been asked of him. He presented his hand, lightly smeared with blood.

"You'll have to wash that well," Professor Mason said. "Did you get cut?" he asked Taylor, checking her face and hands.

Taylor shook her head, but she wasn't sure how to reply. Was she all right? She hadn't been cut, but her arm and shoulder still buzzed from the current that had emanated from the scarab.

"You seem a little dazed, Taylor," Professor Mason observed. "Talk to me."

"My arm and neck are numb," Taylor told him, "and I had the strangest sort of vision."

"A vision?" her father asked.

"I don't know what else you'd call it. A day-dream? But it was so real. I felt as if I were in a desert with the scarab in my hand."

"Hmm," Professor Mason pondered. "I wonder if you're in shock. Do you feel cold or dizzy?"

"No, just . . . just . . . tingly, like I said."

"Let's get you home."

"But what about the three-headed cow?" Taylor reminded her father, trying to smile. She was feeling better every minute as the effects of the scarab wore off.

"I think we've had enough excitement for today," Professor Mason insisted.

• • •

When Taylor and her father walked into their living room, Mrs. Mason rushed in from the kitchen. "Are you two all right? I saw what happened in the museum. It was on TV. I've been calling. Why haven't you been answering your phones?"

"I didn't hear it ring." Professor Mason searched his pockets until he found his phone. "In all the excitement, I wasn't paying attention."

Taylor took her phone from the slim bag she carried over her shoulder. "That's bizarre," she said. The glass on her cell phone screen was cracked in a thousand small lines.

"What happened?" Mrs. Mason asked, looking to Professor Mason with an alarmed expression.

The Masons sat on the living room couch and Professor Mason recounted the events for his wife. "I don't understand how Taylor's phone was cracked," Mrs. Mason said.

Her parents both looked to Taylor for an explanation, but she could only shrug in bewilderment. "Maybe it got fried when that electric shock ran up my body."

"What electric shock?!" Mrs. Mason asked.

Taylor described what had happened to her and how she'd felt transported to Egypt.

Mrs. Mason grew increasingly alarmed as Taylor continued her story. She turned to her husband. "Did Taylor hit her head at any point?"

"I don't think so," he replied.

"No," Taylor said.

"She might have just pinched a nerve," Professor Mason said. "There's not too much the doctors can do for that. It has to get better on its own."

"I'll be fine," Taylor agreed. The numbness was almost all better, even though she suddenly felt like resting. "But I am feeling a little shaky — I mean, we watched a robbery almost happen. I'd like to nap, if that's okay."

"Of course it is," Mrs. Mason said. "But before you go, I have to tell both of you my big news." She looked at her husband and Taylor excitedly.

"The Museum of Egyptian Antiquities in Cairo wants to do a production of *The Journey of Nefertiti* as part of their anniversary gala!"

"That's awesome, Mom!" Taylor cried happily. "You must be so excited!"

"Yes, I am. Actors will perform the play and there's already a director, but they want me to come to oversee it and advise."

"That's great, honey!" Professor Mason said. "I'll go with you. I can use the time to finish the article I'm writing on ancient Egyptian languages. All the research resources I need will be right there."

"That would be wonderful," Mrs. Mason said.

Professor Mason's face lit with excitement. "In fact, there's a group trip being sponsored by the archaeology department at the university. I hadn't wanted to leave you two for such a long time, but if you're heading there it makes sense for all of us to go. I'll make a few phone calls and see if we can be part of it."

"I'm going, too?" Taylor asked hopefully.

"Absolutely!" Professor Mason replied. "You're about to see the pyramids, Taylor!"

"Beyond awesome!" Taylor shouted. This was a dream come true. She could almost feel herself back in the desert from her daydream.

"Do you all want to go out to celebrate?" Professor Mason asked them.

"I'd love to!" Mrs. Mason agreed. "Taylor?"

"I — I'd sort of like to sleep."

"Oh, then we won't —"

"No, Mom, go!" Taylor insisted, smiling. "I'll be totally fine."

4

TAYLOR SLEPT while her phone recharged. When she awoke, she searched for Jason online. Even though he'd been sort of annoying, she was still curious about him.

Luckily, despite the cracks in the glass cover, her phone still functioned. The broken glass made it difficult to see well, but not impossible, and she found him almost instantly.

In his profile picture he was dressed as a

pharaoh, complete with high headdress, heavy medallion, skirt, and high strapped sandals. The caption under the photo read: LAST HALLOWEEN. After debating for a moment, she decided not to submit a "friend" request but simply sent a message instead.

Hi Jason. It's Taylor, from the museum. How's your hand? Message me if you get a chance.

She waited a few minutes to see if he'd respond but no reply came, so she put her phone aside, lay back down on her bed, and fell asleep.

It was early evening and summer's dusky late light filled Taylor's bedroom when she awoke. "Anybody home?" she called, going out into the hallway. When no reply came, she remembered that her parents had gone out.

Taylor called her friend Sharon to tell her

about everything that had happened that day, but only got voice mail.

Gazing down at her cracked phone, she sighed. There was no way she could keep using it in this condition. Taylor remembered an ad that she'd noticed in yesterday's newspaper. It advertised a new store that repaired cell phones and contained a 20-percent-off coupon for new customers. It was just what she needed.

Taylor searched in the living room, kitchen, and family area with no luck. There didn't seem to be a single old newspaper in the entire house.

Then she realized why. "Recycling!" she said out loud. It was tomorrow and her parents had bundled all the old papers to put out on the curb. They always left them in the garage until the morning.

Taylor headed out the back door to the garage, which was a separate building. As she bent to lift the garage door, she heard something buzzing, as though an insect were near her ear.

She swatted at it and the sound retreated into the distance.

Taylor opened the door and stepped in, glancing at the rakes, shovels, lawnmower, and other yard work equipment. There, neatly stacked and tied by the door, as always, sat a week's worth of old newspapers. Yesterday's paper was right on top. Taylor crouched in front of the stack, and as she struggled with the twine knot, she absently swatted away insects that landed on her cheek, hair, and hands.

There were so many of them! She checked around. Was there an insect nest of some kind in the garage?

Once more, Taylor returned to the knot, trying unsuccessfully to open it. This was getting ridiculous! The knot was too tight.

"Ow!" Something had bitten her hand and it really stung.

A black bug about the size of a quarter still sat on her hand. Taylor had never seen anything like it. It had furry wings and sharp teeth. She flung it off.

"I don't believe this!" she cried when the creature stayed affixed to her hand. It gripped her with its tiny feet.

The buzz of insects grew louder and Taylor looked down, following the sound. The floor of the garage was covered with a swarm of the awful bugs.

One of the insects dropped from the ceiling onto her shoulder and Taylor quickly swatted it off. Another fell into her hair, and then another.

Taylor batted at her hair. Panicked, she ran for the open garage door. In another second the insects would be all over her. She had to get to the door.

But just before Taylor reached it, the half-opened door rumbled into motion, hitting the ground as though an invisible hand had slammed it down.

The strange insects swarmed toward Taylor, their buzzing chatter filling her ears. They were moving across the garage floor and over the lawn equipment like an unstoppable tide.

How had so many appeared all at once? Where were they coming from?

"Help!" Taylor shouted as she pulled up on the garage door handle with all her strength. As she opened her mouth, one of the insects dropped onto her tongue, and she spit it out.

The horrible bugs were crawling up her legs. Taylor frantically hit at them. She had to get out of there before they covered her completely.

Desperate to be free of the insects, Taylor wiped her arms and legs. Some of them clung to her hand, and she held it out to see.

The chattering creatures had the fangs and leathery wings of tiny bats!

The bugs on her hand suddenly sprang up and began to bite her face. Horrified, Taylor shut her eyes and stumbled forward blindly, slamming her head on the garage door.

the Egyptian desert, and that couldn't have happened. She studied her hands for signs of a bug bite or scratch but there was nothing.

"How do you feel now?" Professor Mason asked.

"All right. A little confused."

"Do you see any bugs now?" her father went on.

"Of course not! I'm not crazy!"

"And where are we?" Mrs. Mason asked.

"The garage. Obviously!"

They thought she'd really lost it. That much was clear. Were they right? Was she coming unglued?

"We're not in the Egyptian desert?" Mrs. Mason checked.

"Mom!" Taylor cried.

"Well, you are definitely going to see Dr. Seabridge," Mrs. Mason said.

"I'm fine," Taylor insisted.

"You're not fine! You fainted out here in the garage. You're seeing things. That's not my idea of fine," Mrs. Mason told Taylor firmly. "We never should have left you home alone."

Professor Mason helped Taylor get to her feet. "Your mom's right. You have to be checked out. We want you feeling one hundred percent when we go to Egypt."

Taylor smiled at the mention of Egypt.

"We're only going if Taylor is well enough," Mrs. Mason told him.

"Oh, I'll be well enough," Taylor said, getting to her feet. "I'll be totally fine."

• • •

"I'll be great by tomorrow morning," Taylor told her mother for the fifth time as they watched TV together later that evening.

"I hope so, but let's see what the doctor says

tomorrow," her mother replied, as she had four times already. "You're sure you didn't bang your head when you fell?"

"Positive," Taylor replied.

"Because you shouldn't sleep if you've had a bad knock on the head. You might have a concussion."

"I don't!"

"Good. Then you should get to bed after this show. A good night's sleep might help."

Taylor had *no* idea how she would ever get to sleep after her long nap, but her mother insisted.

Upstairs, sitting on the edge of her bed, Taylor looked through her cracked phone screen for any new text messages. Sharon had contacted her to say she was sorry she'd missed Taylor and ask if Taylor could go for a bike ride tomorrow. *KK*. Taylor replied. *Will call you in the a.m.*

Almost a half minute later, Sharon texted back. *K. Check online. You're in my post. So cool!*

Switching apps on her phone, Taylor perused her newsfeed. At about ten items down she came to a TV news clip Sharon had posted. It was taken from the security cameras at the Haunted Museum. It showed the guards tackling Valdry and the cases being overturned. She'd written: *My bestie grabs priceless treasure before thief can get it. You go, girl!*

Taylor replayed the short video, and noticed herself standing next to Jason. She watched as she grabbed the scarab from the floor. But this time she spied something else that she hadn't seen before. The thief, Valdry, was watching her the whole time. And from behind his dark glasses a blast of red had flashed at her.

But the thief's eyes appeared to be normal as the guard pulled off his dark glasses. What had caused that flash of red?

Was it simply a case of photographic red-eye?

Taylor watched the clip again. Yes! The red was there. Definitely! This time she also noticed that a blank faraway expression had come across her face as she stood there. It was as though she was in a hypnotic trance. That must have been when she was seeing herself in the Egyptian desert.

The phone buzzed and a message from Jason appeared. *Hand OK, thanx. Saw the news clip you're tagged in. That guy look sketchy to you? What's with his red eyes?*

Right? Taylor responded. *I thought I was imagining it! What is that?*

No idea!!

"Taylor!" Mrs. Mason called from the first floor. "Are you awake?"

"Yeah, I am," she replied, opening her door.

"Come down. You're on the local news," Mrs. Mason said.

Turn on channel 12. We're on. Taylor texted as she headed out of her room.

Taylor joined her family in the living room where they sat in front of the TV set. The same news clip Sharon had posted was playing on the TV. "Watch this guy's eyes," Taylor said excitedly as she slipped onto the couch in between her parents. "Do you see them flash red?"

Both Taylor and her parents leaned forward intently as the clip played. "They did flash!" Mrs. Mason cried.

"No, that was just a reflection," Professor Mason disagreed.

But Taylor sided with her mom. His eyes had definitely flashed.

6

In the morning, Taylor awoke around ten when something beside her buzzed. Turning her head she saw the blue scarab, and scrambled up to sit. It looked *exactly* like the scarab she'd touched in the Haunted Museum.

Bzzzz!

Taylor slid back on her bed, away from the blue scarab.

How was it making that sound?

Tossing back her covers, Taylor hurried to her closet to grab a shoebox from the floor. She emptied out one of the new sandals inside it and grabbed the other.

With her sandal in one hand and the empty box in the other, Taylor approached the scarab on the bed.

Bzzzz!

Was it alive or just a blue carved stone? The buzzing had to mean it was alive, didn't it?

The memory of the swarming insects in the garage made Taylor even more nervous. She checked around the room. So far she didn't see any more of the bugs.

Steeling her nerves, Taylor used the sandal to scoop the scarab into the box, quickly covering it. *Bzzzz!* The scarab was still buzzing inside the shoebox.

Taylor placed the box on her bed and stepped back.

She stared at it. Now what?

"Mom!" Taylor shouted. "Dad! Come here. Quick!"

Inside the box the scarab buzzed again.

Taylor left the shoebox on the bed and went to look for her parents. On the chest at the bottom of the stairs she found a note: *Dad's at the university. I just went next door. Didn't want to wake you. Call if you need me.*

She needed her mother, all right!

Taylor's phone was upstairs so she went back to get it. There was a text message from Sharon: *Ready to go?* At once Taylor remembered the bike ride she'd planned with her friend the day before. The phone alerted her of another incoming text. Again it was from Sharon. *Let's ride to the Haunted*

Museum. I want to see where all the excitement happened.

Taylor wasn't sure what she should do. If her parents thought she wasn't well — or was in a state of shock — they might cancel the trip to Egypt. She really, *really* didn't want that to happen.

The buzzing in the shoebox had stopped. That was a good sign. She stood listening a moment longer, just to be sure. Silence.

The new quiet gave Taylor the nerve to lift the shoebox carefully from the bed. Maybe she could put it in her bike basket and ride the scarab over to the Haunted Museum. They'd be happy to have it back, and she wouldn't need to be alone in the house with the blue carving for a minute longer than necessary.

OK, come on over, she texted Sharon.

7

Sharon sat on her bike and pushed back her dark curls as Taylor placed the shoebox, which she'd put into a paper bag, into the basket of her own bike. "What's in there?" Sharon asked.

"Somehow a scarab from the Nefertiti collection followed me home," Taylor replied as she secured the bag with a bungee cord.

"What?!" Sharon's eyes widened in alarm. "You stole something from the exhibit?"

Taylor looked up sharply. "No! No way!" She looked around, panicked. What if someone heard Sharon say that? "I would never!"

"Then what happened?"

"I don't know! It just appeared in my room."

Sharon squinted skeptically at Taylor.

"Really! I don't know how it got there."

Pursing her lips thoughtfully, Sharon considered the question. "Maybe someone slipped the scarab into your pocket, and it fell out when you weren't looking."

"My sundress *does* have pockets." Taylor liked this logical explanation. "But who would do that?"

Sharon shrugged helplessly.

"And why?" Taylor asked.

"Maybe that Jason kid you met used you to smuggle it out," Sharon suggested.

That didn't sound right to Taylor. Jason didn't seem like a thief. "I don't think so," she said.

"Besides, I put the thing back into the security guard's box. How could it have gotten out?"

"Who knows?"

Taylor got onto her bike. "Let's just ride over to the Haunted Museum to return it."

Sharon began to pedal in the direction of the museum and Taylor followed. After about fifteen minutes, when the Haunted Museum came into view, Taylor began to feel relieved. Soon this weird blue scarab would be back where it belonged.

"I think it's closed," Sharon called over her shoulder as she glided to a stop at the front of the building.

Taylor pulled up alongside Sharon. There was a padlock on the door and all the signs were gone, except one: CLOSED UNTIL FURTHER NOTICE.

"Oh no!" Taylor wailed.

"We could take it to the police," Sharon said.

"What if they think I stole it?"

"Maybe they wouldn't care, as long as you're returning it."

Taylor wasn't confident it would be that easy.

Sharon pointed to the front door. "Someone's moving around inside."

Taylor and Sharon got off their bikes right away and banged on the front door. "Hello? Hello?" Taylor called.

"Can I help you?" Taylor and Sharon both jumped, startled when someone behind them spoke.

The woman was tall and thin with very pale skin. Short black hair peeked out from under a head wrap of frayed cloth that reminded Taylor of a mummy. Painted-on eyebrows arched over her dark glasses.

"What do you need?" she asked.

The woman smelled strongly of something familiar. Sunblock? Maybe that was why she was so pale.

"Do you work for the museum?" Sharon asked the woman.

"Yes," she replied.

There was something creepy about her, Taylor decided, and it was more than her appearance. Maybe it was her harsh voice, or her quick, jerky movements. But before Taylor could make up her mind, Sharon lifted the shoebox from Taylor's basket and thrust it toward the woman. "Here! We came to give you this."

It happened so fast, Taylor couldn't be sure — but she was nearly certain that she heard buzzing from the box. And that a spark of red flashed behind the woman's dark sunglasses.

"Okay, then," Sharon said brightly, pushing off on her bike. "You'll be sure to get that scarab back to where it belongs?"

Taylor was still staring at the woman's sunglasses, hoping they'd flash again so she could be sure she'd really seen it. They were so black that Taylor couldn't find the woman's eyes behind them at all.

"It's as good as done," the woman said quietly.

"Come on, Taylor!"

With a nod to the woman, Taylor joined her friend. "At least that's taken care of," Sharon said as they cycled off together away from the museum. "See? No police, no getting in trouble."

"Yeah," Taylor said, glancing back over her shoulder for one last look at the strange woman. But she was too late. The woman was gone.

LATER THAT afternoon, Dr. Seabridge looked at Taylor from across her large desk. She had just finished giving Taylor a physical. "I see no sign of concussion," she said. "But the fact that you're being followed by strange bugs concerns me."

Taylor noticed her parents, who sat beside her, exchange a quick, worried glance. Obviously they'd spoken to the doctor about the odd things that had happened. "I haven't seen them for a long time," she replied quickly, which was true. Ever since she'd returned the scarab to the museum that morning, nothing odd had occurred.

"And no more vivid daydreams of ancient Egypt?" Dr. Seabridge checked.

"Not like the kind I had right after going to the museum, no. I mean, I've been thinking a lot about going to Egypt because I'm excited and all, but that's different."

"Yes, of course, it is."

Mrs. Mason turned toward Taylor. "You'd tell us if you were experiencing any other strange events, wouldn't you?"

"I totally would!" Taylor replied. "Nothing has happened. It's been boring, even."

Professor Mason sat back in the chair, seeming relieved. "Boring is good."

"Well, that's me," Taylor said cheerfully. "Bored as can be."

Dr. Seabridge laughed lightly. "Okay, then. I'd say you're good to go to Egypt."

Taylor wanted to stand up and cheer, pump her fists, and dance around the room. She'd been so worried that the doctor would say she wasn't up to the trip. But she stayed in her seat and smiled calmly, not daring to do anything that might be considered odd behavior.

"But keep an eye on Taylor, just in case," Dr. Seabridge added as the family was about to leave.

• • •

"I'm so glad we're all going on this trip," Taylor's mother said a week later as the Masons pulled out of their driveway and headed to the airport for their 10:00 a.m. flight to Cairo.

Professor Mason turned the car onto the street. "It was so lucky for us that a family canceled at the last minute and we were able to take their spots."

"I can't believe this is really happening," Mrs. Mason added.

"Neither can I," Taylor said. During the week that had just passed, Taylor felt like a goldfish in a bowl, constantly being watched by her parents. "I'm fine!" she'd wanted to shout more than once, but didn't want to seem moody or irritable.

Finally, the waiting was over.

She was on her way to Egypt, and there had been no more buzzing or bugs or visions. The most exciting thing that had happened was finding the place that fixed cell phones and having her screen replaced.

Everything was just great!

At the airport, Taylor checked her big suitcase but kept her backpack for the flight.

"Hey, Taylor," her father said as they stood in the security line. He nodded at someone behind them in line. "Isn't that the young man we met at the Haunted Museum?"

Following the direction of his glance, Taylor saw Jason standing with a blond woman, who, based on the resemblance, appeared to be his mother.

He hadn't told her he was going on this trip. She crossed over to him. "Surprise!" she said with a grin when he noticed her.

Taylor hadn't seen Jason since the day of the near-robbery, but they'd texted back and forth. Taylor had told him about the strange scarab, and all of a sudden she wondered if maybe she'd freaked him out with all the strange things that had been happening. "You're on this trip?" Taylor asked. "Why didn't you say anything when I mentioned that I was going?"

Jason shrugged. "I thought it would be funny to just appear out of nowhere. Mom runs these trips for the university," he said, nodding toward the blond woman in front of him. "We go just about every year."

"That's so cool!" Taylor said. "So how does it work? Does the group split up and send people into different cities, or is it one big happy family?"

Jason nodded. "The whole group stays together."

"Nice." Jason had seemed so stiff at the museum. She hadn't even been sure she liked him all that much. But Taylor felt like they'd sort of become friends after the robbery and texting. It might be fun to have him there, especially since he knew his way around Cairo and shared her enthusiasm for it.

Taylor's parents moved back in line to join them. Professor Mason introduced Jason's mother, Helen, to his wife, and the adults were soon talking eagerly about going to the Egyptian temples near ancient Luxor.

The line inched forward and soon Taylor was ready to pass through the scanner booth. This part always made her nervous even though she wasn't wearing any jewelry and had emptied the coins from her pockets into the bin that held her backpack.

With a deep breath, Taylor stepped into the booth when the security guard on the other side waved her forward.

The moment she was inside, a piercing alarm blared, and Taylor cringed.

"Step forward, young lady," a stern-faced female agent commanded her from the far side of the scanner booth. Only then did Taylor realize that *she* was the cause of the commotion.

Taylor's mom stepped toward the booth, but a security guard detained her.

The agent waved a detection wand along Taylor's arms. "Anything in your pockets?" she asked.

"I don't think so," Taylor replied. She patted the front pockets of her jeans, then the back. "Wait!"

Taylor's eyes widened as she pulled the blue scarab from her back pocket.

The guard's wand buzzed excitedly. She took the scarab from Taylor. "Here's our problem," she said. "It looks like stone, but there must be some kind of metal inside it. Otherwise, it wouldn't have set off the alarm."

The guard handed the scarab to Taylor. "No, you can keep it," Taylor said, stepping back.

"No, here," the guard insisted, pressing it into Taylor's hand. "It's yours."

The scarab buzzed in Taylor's hand, just as it had before. The tingling ran up her arm and along the back of her neck. Her whole body felt numb as she stumbled forward to lift her backpack off the security conveyor belt.

Someone came to stand at her shoulder, and Taylor turned her face toward the setting red sun. The desert sands before her shone with pinkish light.

"Are you all right?"

"I am more truly myself than ever, my pharaoh."

"What did you just say?" Jason asked.

Taylor blinked. The busy airport was once more all around her, the garbled announcements and rattling of suitcase wheels and the chatter of people in the duty-free shop nearby. She was still clenching the scarab in her palm. Quickly, she slipped it into her back pocket and in the next second, Taylor's parents were at her side.

"What set off the alarm?" Professor Mason asked.

What would he think if she showed him the scarab in her pocket? He would have to believe that she stole it. What other possible explanation could there be? She couldn't explain what it was doing there. Sharon had definitely handed the shoebox to that creepy woman back at the Haunted Museum. Then how had it gotten into her pocket?

"You look a little blank there, kiddo," her father said. "Sure you're okay?"

"Maybe this isn't a good idea," her mother added. "We can still go home."

"No! No way!" Taylor said, panicking. "I just had some coins in my pocket that set off the alarm. I'm fine."

"Are you sure?" Taylor's mother asked, smoothing her daughter's hair behind her ear.

"Totally," Taylor answered. "I just got a little scared is all. It's embarrassing to be pulled out of line in front of everybody."

Mrs. Mason rubbed her back. "It happens to everybody sometimes. It's nothing to worry about."

"I'll just have some water," Taylor said, pointing to a nearby drinking fountain.

At the fountain she sipped the water and wondered what she should do. The scarab was a priceless treasure.

She wanted to tell someone, but who would believe her?

The world had lived without it for thousands of years. What would a few more centuries matter?

Lifting her head, she spied an airport trash bin to her right. Taylor veered toward it on her way back to her mother and the others, and — with a quick motion she hoped no one saw — she dropped the scarab into the can.

9

TAYLOR GAZED out the cab window at the busy, crowded streets of Cairo. Even though it would have been ten at night if they were home, it was only five thirty in the afternoon there in Cairo because of the time zone change.

The bus that the university had provided to pick the group up had been overly crowded, so Taylor and her parents were sharing the taxi with Jason and his mother on the way to their hotel.

Their driver was dressed in a long, white cotton robe and a brimless, round, white cap, and he sat silent and unsmiling in the barely moving traffic.

It seemed to Taylor that, in many ways, Cairo was like any other large, modern city. The airport had been slightly chaotic, and Taylor had liked her delicious falafel-and-hummus-in-pita-bread snack. She'd bought a small jade elephant as a souvenir for Sharon, and several postcards featuring the pyramids and the sphinx to send.

In the city itself, tall apartment buildings were mixed in among skyscrapers, restaurants, and smaller businesses. Many women had their heads covered with scarves and wore long-sleeved dresses, and the people on the streets wore a combination of traditional and modern clothing.

Taylor suddenly had an odd, but strong, sensation that someone was looking at her. Scanning the crowds on the sidewalk, she searched for the person who might be staring her way.

She locked eyes with a scruffy young man. His white shirt and dark pants were dirty and he wore sunglasses. Although his messy hair was nearly black, his skin was so pale it was almost white.

"What's wrong, Taylor?" Mrs. Mason asked.

"There's a man on the street who's staring at me," Taylor replied.

"Where?" Jason asked, leaning toward her to look out the window.

Before Taylor could answer, the man left the sidewalk and wove his way through the unmoving traffic. "He's coming toward our cab!" Taylor cried, alarmed.

With a *click*, the driver locked the doors.

From seemingly out of nowhere, other pale,

bedraggled men and women walked among the cars, heading toward the cab.

All of them wore very dark sunglasses.

"What's going on?" Professor Mason asked the cabdriver. The man only shrugged his shoulders in response, but beads of sweat had popped out on his forehead.

The strange people surrounded the car. Some even climbed onto the hood and stared in through the front windshield. Others were on the trunk, peering in through the back.

The driver leaned on his horn, banging on the front window and shouting at them, "Go away!"

Terrified, Taylor could only stare, wide-eyed.

"Get out of here!" Jason yelled at them as he took Taylor's hand protectively.

One of the men pushed closer to press his cheek against the glass.

That was when Taylor saw the tiny, black bat-like insect that hung on a cord at his neck. It was the exact size and shape as the ones that had attacked her in the garage.

"I don't have it!" Taylor shouted, not knowing exactly why. "I don't have it!"

From behind their sunglasses, flashes of red popped.

"Call the police," Mrs. Mason said, leaning toward their driver.

A sudden shrill whistle made Taylor wince.

In the next instant, she could see only white. It was as if someone had flashed a light right into her eyes, blinding her.

What was happening?

In the moments of silence that followed the flash, Taylor waited for something awful to happen. Hunched and tense, she squeezed her eyelids together and clenched Jason's hand. He gripped it back.

After a few tense moments of silence, the noise from the street began to filter through again, normal sounds of traffic and people outside.

Cautiously, Taylor peered out through narrowed eyes. The strange people were gone.

"What just happened?" Professor Mason asked the driver.

"It is time for you all to go," he said in heavily accented English.

"But we're not at the hotel yet," Jason's mother said.

"It is very close, down that block. Go now!" the driver insisted. Getting quickly out of the car, he ran to the back and opened the trunk.

"I think he's taking our suitcases out," Mrs. Mason said.

Professor Mason hurried out of the cab. Taylor heard him arguing with the driver. Her father reappeared at the back window, waving for them all to get out.

All of their luggage was in the road and the driver had hopped back into the driver's seat of the cab. With his horn blaring, he pushed his vehicle forward through traffic, forcing other cars and trucks to let him through.

"Let's go, then," Professor Mason said. The traffic barely moved, so it wasn't too hard to weave between the vehicles with their things. When they'd carried all the suitcases to the sidewalk, they stood looking at one another.

Jason spoke first. "What just happened?"

"Those people looked like the thieves at the Haunted Museum exhibit," Taylor said. "They were all pale and wearing sunglasses."

"That's true," Jason said.

"What did they want?" Mrs. Mason asked.

"To rob us," Jason's mother said. "What a shame. I've heard of gangs here that target tourists, but it hasn't happened to one of our university groups yet."

Her parents nodded, but Taylor didn't think Helen was right — at least not completely. Those strange people were after something, and Taylor was pretty sure it wasn't money. There were people on the street who would have been easier to rob.

They thought she still had the blue scarab from the Haunted Museum collection. That had to be it.

But how did they even know she was in Cairo?

IT HAD been a very long trip, and by the time the Masons finally reached the hotel that the university had booked for the school group, all Taylor wanted was to go to sleep.

"You take this pull-out bed in the main room," Mrs. Mason said, pointing to the sofa bed that had already been prepared for her by the hotel staff. "We'll be in the room here if you need anything."

Taylor nodded and tossed her suitcase on the bed.

Professor Mason kissed the top of Taylor's head. "Good night, kiddo. See you in the morning."

" 'Night," Taylor replied as he disappeared into the bedroom.

Mrs. Mason sat on the edge of the sofa bed. "How are you holding up?" she asked.

Taylor nodded. "Okay. You?"

"Nervous about my play," Mrs. Mason admitted. "I meet the people from the Egyptian Museum tomorrow."

"Don't worry," Taylor said, sitting beside her mother. "They already love the play, and they'll love you, too."

Mrs. Mason squeezed Taylor's hand and smiled.

"Sweet dreams," her mother said from the doorway. From inside Taylor could hear her father's snores.

Taylor stretched toward her suitcase to get out her pajamas. It felt as though she'd been in the same shorts and T-shirt forever. It would feel good to wash up and change.

But when she placed her hand on her suitcase, she stopped.

A low hum came from the bag.

She'd brought her computer. Maybe it had somehow turned itself on?

Still, it made her uneasy. It sounded just like . . .

Carefully, Taylor unzipped the top of the suitcase and slowly lifted it open.

Hundreds of the same chattering black bat bugs swarmed from the suitcase, emitting a deafening sound, and Taylor scrambled away from the bed.

"Mom! Dad! Mom!"

Her parents appeared at the bedroom door, horrified expressions on their faces.

Taylor screamed as the creatures began to climb up her legs.

11

Taylor slumped over on a worn purple velvet couch in the lobby. She couldn't stop rubbing her bare legs. Even though her parents had swatted the batlike insects off as they fled the room, she had the sensation that they were still crawling on her. Above her, flickering electric bulbs on chandeliers were meant to give the impression of candlelight but simply imparted a disquieting feeling to the otherwise dimly lit lobby.

Across the way, she could hear her parents arguing with the clerk at the front desk, who claimed that there was no insect problem at the hotel. Taylor felt sorry for him because she suspected that what he said was true. Those bat insects had come from her suitcase, not the walls.

Had she brought those creepy bugs with her from home? But they hadn't been in her suitcase at the airport. Wouldn't security have found them?

"Well, there's a swarm of bugs in the room, and we can't sleep there tonight," Professor Mason told the clerk, his voice rising angrily. "You have to find us another room."

"But there is no other room," the desk clerk argued.

"Then find us a room at another hotel," Mrs. Mason said.

Taylor felt a poke on her arm and turned quickly. A child of about eight with long, silky black hair wearing a dark purple caftan sat on the couch beside Taylor.

But Taylor hadn't noticed her enter the lobby. Where had she come from?

The girl gazed up at Taylor, saying something in a language Taylor didn't know.

"Sorry. I don't know what you're saying."

The girl cupped her hand and presented it, but Taylor just shook her head, frustrated that she couldn't understand.

Taking a pad and pen from a nearby table, she drew a circle, and then filled in the wings, pincers, and antennae of the scarab.

The scarab?!

With large, expectant eyes, the girl looked up at Taylor, waiting.

How did she know about the scarab? Who was this girl? Why was she out after midnight?

Taylor gazed around the lobby but saw no one who appeared to be her parent.

When Taylor turned back to the girl, she was gazing off toward an elevator across the far side of the lobby, almost as if waiting for someone. But something about her had changed. Her face seemed lined, and dark circles had formed under her eyes. Her cheeks sagged. Rather than a sweet young girl, she looked more like a haggard, very old woman.

As if she felt Taylor's eyes studying her, the little girl snapped her head around to face Taylor.

The dark, peering eyes were sunk deep into a wrinkled, shriveled face.

And in the next second — she was a child again.

Had it been a trick of the flickering light? Or maybe her jet lag and fatigue were making her imagination go wild.

"All right! They've found us another room," Professor Mason announced, heading toward Taylor with Mrs. Mason at his side.

"There are two bedrooms, which is good news. We'll just need to share a bathroom with some other guests down the hall," Mrs. Mason added.

Taylor stood and the girl scampered behind her. "Don't be scared," Taylor told her. "It's just my parents."

"Who are you talking to?" Taylor's father asked.

"This little girl who —" Taylor glanced behind her, but there was no one there. Where had she gone? "She was here a second ago."

"Oh well," Mrs. Mason said with a shrug. "I'm exhausted. Let's go to our new room." She checked the key card the manager had given her. "It's room three-thirteen. They're bringing our bags over now. We have to take this small elevator at the end of this hall."

Taylor followed them, still searching for the little girl. As she checked over her shoulder, she saw the pad on which the child had drawn the scarab lying on the hotel carpet. "Go ahead," she said to her parents as she hurried back into the lobby to get it. "I'll be right up."

"Don't be long," her father said.

As Taylor stooped to pick up the paper, she noticed a light coming from the lobby elevator. Its doors were slowly closing, but she was able to see a tall man in dark glasses holding the hand of the girl who had spoken to her.

She knew the man, had seen him before. She was sure of it!

Valdry! He was the man who had tried to steal the scarab from the Haunted Museum.

Taylor hurried to the main desk. "Excuse me," she said to the manager.

The manager noticed her and approached. "How can I be of assistance?"

"I thought I should tell you that I just saw a man who's a wanted thief. He steals ancient treasures, and he's right here in your hotel." Taylor pointed to the elevator. "He just went upstairs with a little girl."

Laughter twinkled in the manager's eyes. "You must mean Dr. Valdry and his daughter, Simone."

"Yes!" Taylor cried. "That's him! You should call the police."

"Dr. Valdry is one of our oldest customers. When he's in Cairo he always stays here. I'm sure you're mistaken about him."

"I'm not. The police are after him."

The manager's expression became impatient. "I will be certain to inform the proper authorities of your concern," he said, but his stiff tone told Taylor that he had no intention of telling anyone anything.

"Thank you," Taylor said, even though she didn't believe him.

The manager bowed slightly from the waist. "Not at all."

Taylor rode the elevator to the third floor and found room thirteen. It was a plain room but a bigger suite, and Taylor was happy to have a bedroom to herself. Her mother was still in the small kitchenette area, waiting for her daughter. "Everything all right?" she asked.

Taylor quickly told her mother everything that had happened. "I'm sure it's the same guy, Mom."

"Well, you reported it to the hotel," her mother said. "What else can you do?"

"But what if he comes after me because he thinks I have the scarab?" Taylor asked. She thought of the terrifying people who surrounded the cab that day.

"You don't have it, do you?" Mrs. Mason asked.

"No," Taylor said.

Right now it was sitting in a trash bin at John F. Kennedy International Airport in New York. She'd put it there herself.

"If you see him again, let us know right away," Mrs. Mason said. "Now get some rest."

Exhausted though she was, Taylor couldn't sleep. Her mind raced with memories of everything that had happened — the attempted robbery at the Haunted Museum, Valdry with his flashing sunglasses, the vision of the desert, the swarming beetles. She'd thought coming to Egypt would put her far away from everything that had happened, but there'd been the pale people who had surrounded the cab, the strange little girl, the scarab. It all seemed so unreal.

Tossing back and forth on the bed until the sheets were a tangle at her feet, Taylor couldn't settle down.

Her mother would go to the Egyptian Museum in Cairo tomorrow. Taylor decided to ask if she could go along. Maybe she could learn something there that would make sense of all that had happened. If she could figure out what was happening, maybe she could stop it.

I WISH I was going to the museum with you," Jason said that morning when the group met for breakfast. "My mom insists I go for a ride down the Nile with her today."

"That sounds like fun," Taylor said as she spooned a breakfast of yogurt, honey, and almonds into her mouth. "I'd like to go with you but I want to see what I can find out at the museum. Something very weird is going on."

She told him about the bugs in her suitcase and the strange old-young girl and seeing Valdry.

"That man you saw — are you sure it was Valdry?"

"I'm positive."

The Masons joined Taylor and Jason at the table, carrying cups of coffee. "Ready to go?" Professor Mason asked Taylor.

"You're coming, too?" Taylor asked.

Professor Mason grinned with delight. "Half the students are coming, too. I have a real treat planned for us. I contacted the head curator at the museum, Dr. Ardath Bey —"

"He's the man who helped Belladonna Bloodstone get the exhibit of Nefertiti's treasures at the Haunted Museum, remember?" Taylor said.

"Oh? Is he?" Professor Mason asked. Clearly he didn't approve. "Well, as a professional courtesy, he's going to give us a private showing of items on loan from the Egyptian Museum in Berlin, Germany."

"That famous bust of Nefertiti is in Berlin," Jason said.

"Not right now, it's not," Professor Mason said.

"We're going to see the real thing?" Taylor asked, growing excited.

Mr. and Mrs. Mason nodded excitedly. "Let's go!" Taylor cried. This was something she'd always wanted to see. The thought of it made her throw off her worry and jet lag.

"You have to tell me all about it," Jason said. "Take pictures."

"If I'm allowed to I will," Taylor promised, grabbing her daypack and pushing back her chair.

• • •

The Egyptian Museum in Cairo was a huge, red stone building that took up blocks. Taylor and her parents climbed the wide steps and passed through the arched entryway. The inside was cool and sunny, lit by sunlight beaming through the large skylight on the roof. The first floor was two stories high with a balcony that wrapped around the second floor and reached another two stories.

At the inside front entrance, two uniformed guards checked the handbags and backpacks of the people entering. After they searched Mrs. Mason's straw purse, Taylor presented the day-pack she had slung over her shoulders.

"What are you carrying this marker for?" the guard asked, lifting a thick black marker from her pack.

"I forgot that was even in there," Taylor said. "I was using it to make posters back at school."

"I'll have to take it," the guard said. "We can't risk anyone marking up the artwork."

"I would never!" Taylor cried, horrified by the idea.

The guard smiled.

"Yes, take the marker. Definitely take it," Taylor said as the guard went back to searching the rest of her bag before returning it to her.

Taylor caught up to her parents in line.

"The guard thought I was going to ruin the art with my marker," she told them. "Who would do that?"

"Better to be safe than sorry," Professor Mason said.

They stepped inside the museum. In the center of the lobby were two huge statues of a seated pharaoh and his queen. Taylor and her parents were moving toward it when a man stepped in their path.

"Professor Mason?"

The man was very tall and dressed in a long, white cotton robe and wearing a rounded red tassled hat called a fez. He had white, short hair and a deeply lined face. When he spoke, his voice was deep, almost soothing. "I am Ardath Bey." He extended his arm to shake Professor Mason's hand. "You contacted me about the Berlin treasures."

Professor Mason shook his hand and introduced Mrs. Mason and Taylor. Dr. Bey beckoned for them to follow him through the museum, past gigantic statues of pharaohs and queens, reconstructed temples, and hundreds of glass cases housing items from ancient Egypt, some from royal palaces, others simple everyday items from common life.

"A lot different from the Haunted Museum, wouldn't you say?" Professor Mason kidded Taylor.

Dr. Bey took a key from his pocket and unlocked a door. When they were inside he locked it once again.

In the center of the room, inside a glass case, was the bust of Nefertiti. Taylor gasped, and then chewed her lip as she walked toward it, drawn to the head-and-shoulder likeness of the queen.

Mrs. Mason said, coming alongside Taylor, "We're getting a special sneak peek, thanks to Dr. Bey, since I have to leave early for the play rehearsal. The others from our group will get to see it later this afternoon. Breathtaking isn't it?"

Breathtaking was the exact right word, Taylor thought, because she was so awed by the statue that she couldn't speak, could barely breathe. Nefertiti's beauty was undeniable, but it was more than that. So much strength, power, and inner life were expressed on her face.

Dr. Bey lifted something heavy from a drawer

and placed it on the table. "Could that gold plate really be what I think it is?" Professor Mason asked, clearly amazed.

"Akhenaten and Nefertiti with their children under the rays of Aten," Dr. Bey said.

Taylor studied the picture etched into the tile. A man and woman sat facing each other. They wore identical cone-shaped crowns. They held five children in their arms and on their laps. Above them was a sun disc with twelve rays beaming down on the royal couple and their children.

"Why do the people look so strange?" Taylor asked Dr. Bey. "The style is so different from other ancient Egyptian artwork I've seen. The children just look like shrunken adults. The sun even resembles some kind of machine."

Dr. Bey's eyes betrayed a quickly shifting emotion. Taylor could tell he was affected by her words, but what was he thinking?

Suddenly from within her pack, Taylor's phone buzzed and began playing "Walk Like an Egyptian" by the Bangles. She'd selected the ringtone especially for the trip and thought it was funny. But now it suddenly seemed embarrassing.

Quickly pulling open her bag, she grabbed for her phone. It was Jason. She declined the call and put the phone back inside her pack. "Sorry," she said.

When she looked back to Dr. Bey, he was staring at her phone in her bag. Was he thinking she was rude for not having shut it off? Had she embarrassed her parents in front of Dr. Bey?

"You were saying about the Amarna period artwork?" Dr. Bey reminded her.

"Oh yeah — just that I think it's so weird looking."

"It's a style of art unique to the reign of

Akhenaten. It's not seen before or after their rule," he explained. "This is one in a series of tiles."

"I thought those treasures were on loan to the Haunted Museum," Taylor said.

Dr. Bey rolled his eyes. "How that Bloodstone woman talked me into allowing it, I'll never understand."

"I know!" Professor Mason cried. "She told us you owed her a favor."

"Don't remind me," Dr. Bey said. "At any rate, the remaining tiles have never been seen and no one knows where they are."

From the pocket of her shorts, Mrs. Mason's cell phone buzzed. She took it out and read the text. "They're ready to meet me in the museum theater," she told them.

"Dr. Bey and I are going to be looking over some pieces from the collection, to see what we can make of this style of hieroglyphics," Professor

Mason said. "I'll catch up with you two in the theater."

"Okay. Dr. Bey, thank you so much for inviting us to see the statue! Come on, Taylor."

"I'll have to let you out," Dr. Bey said, lifting his key.

"Dr. Bey, what do you think of the theories regarding Smenkhkare?" Taylor's mom asked as he unlocked the door. "My husband doesn't believe them."

Dr. Bey looked at her sharply, then turned toward Taylor. "What do *you* think of Smenkhkare?"

"Me? I don't know who that is."

Mrs. Mason stepped forward. "The ancient Egyptian records report that Queen Nefertiti died in the twelfth year of her husband Pharaoh Akhenaten's rule, but no one has found her mummy or her tomb," she explained. "Shortly after Nefertiti's supposed death, though, a man named Smenkhkare showed up and became very close to the pharaoh. He was an adviser and lived at the palace. It was very mysterious."

"What's so mysterious about that?" Taylor asked.

"Many people believe that Nefertiti and Akhenaten convinced their subjects that the queen had died but she was really alive, disguised as Smenkhkare."

"Nobody is certain Smenkhkare was really Nefertiti. It's only a theory," Professor Mason said.

"I believe it," Dr. Bey told them. "It allowed Nefertiti to rule even after the pharaoh died, which she did for twelve more years after Akhenaten's death. It makes sense."

Mrs. Mason nodded. "That's something I'd like to add to my play. I think it's very interesting."

"It is," Taylor agreed. The idea that Smenkhkare was Nefertiti disguised as a man was very cool.

Dr. Bey nodded as he stepped away from the door. "Indeed, a very possible theory."

"Oh, that's great!" Mrs. Mason said. "We have to hurry, Taylor, I don't want to be late to meet the cast and director. Maybe there's still time to add to my play."

Dr. Bey stood holding the door open for them. He studied Taylor with a serious intensity. "Good-bye, Dr. Bey," she said as she followed her mother out the door.

"I'm sure we will meet again," Dr. Bey said.

13

THE THEATER in the museum was brightly lit. Sound-proofing tiles were hung in pyramid shapes on the auditorium walls, and thick purple curtains hung onstage. When Taylor and her mother arrived, the ten-person cast and the director rushed to greet them, smiling, shaking hands, and introducing themselves.

"I'm so glad that you're here. We are eager to start, Ashley," the director said to Mrs. Mason.

Her name was Nevin and she was a slim woman, dressed in a black shirt and jeans, with her dark hair pulled back into a bun. "We're still on script but we've read through the play together. Today I'd like to walk through the play and have you suggest any changes you think we need."

"I do have some new ideas, even after just a couple days in this gorgeous city," Mrs. Mason said. "Is it all right if I add a whole new scene, or even two?"

"Whatever you like," Nevin replied. "We want the play to be as wonderful as it can be."

Mrs. Mason smiled. "Great! I can't believe I'll be seeing my play performed here!" She turned to Taylor. "This will be your first chance to see the play performed in a genuine Egyptian setting. Watch and let me know what you think."

"Okay."

Nevin turned down the lights in the audience as Taylor took a seat in the fifth row. Her mother and Nevin sat on the edge of the stage while the actors began with their scripts in their hands.

A young man and woman stepped forward, center stage, and began to read. "Feel the sun, Nefertiti, my love," the young man read. "Here is where we'll build our new kingdom. I will call it Akhetaten."

"Akhetaten," the actress playing Nefertiti repeated. "Horizon of the Aten. A perfect name." The actress lifted her hands up. "Here we will worship the Aten, the sun disc."

"Yes," the pharaoh actor said. "Our people will forget their old gods and goddesses. In this new capital city, the Aten will be worshipped above all others."

The actor playing Pharaoh Akhenaten put his

script down and spoke to Mrs. Mason. "I thought the kingdom was called Amarna, why do you call it Akhetaten?"

"It's the name the ancients used. The name Amarna came later, after the kingdom had been abandoned," Mrs. Mason explained.

The actress playing Nefertiti stepped forward. "Does anyone know what caused Akhenaten and Nefertiti to start this new religion?"

Mrs. Mason shook her head. "Not really. Some scholars think it was a trend toward a more scientific view of the universe. Maybe they were thinking about the movement of the earth, and the seasons, and how life depended on having the sun. But no one is really certain."

The actors continued with the play. Taylor sat forward watching, finding it all fascinating. She was so intent on listening and watching that she gasped when she realized someone was sitting beside her in the darkened theater.

"Dr. Bey!" Taylor cried softly.

"Sorry to startle you, my dear."

The light from the stage threw dark circles under Dr. Bey's eyes and deepened the lines of his face.

"Where's my father?" Taylor asked. "Is he all right?"

"He's happy as a clam poring over ancient manuscripts. He's right where I left him, in my office."

"Should I tell my mother you're here?"

"No," Dr. Bey said. "I came here hoping to speak with you."

"Me?"

"Nefertiti calls to you, doesn't she?" Dr. Bey said.

"She's so beautiful and interesting," Taylor agreed with a nod. "I want to know everything about her."

"You already do know — but you've forgotten."

"I don't understand." What could he mean by that?

"You know about reincarnation, don't you, Taylor?"

Taylor had read enough about ancient Egypt to know. "It's the idea that after death a person's spirit can be reborn into another body," she replied.

"Exactly. Through the centuries Nefertiti has been reborn many times. Sometimes she has been a princess, other times a movie star or a powerful ruler," Dr. Bey said.

"Interesting," Taylor said. "I wonder who she is now."

Dr. Bey bowed his head. Why was he doing

that? Then a startling idea occurred to her and her eyes widened with the shocking understanding.

But surely he was mistaken!

"You don't mean *me*, do you?" Taylor asked softly.

Dr. Bey lifted his eyes to stare at her. "Your Highness."

"No! No! You're wrong. I'm no princess or politician."

"Not yet, but you're young. Who knows what the future will bring? You have already been born into a family that reveres the Egyptian ancients, and you share that interest. You are a perfect choice for Nefertiti's traveling spirit."

"You're joking, right?" she said.

Dr. Bey shook his head. "I recognized you the moment you appeared in the museum. Those eyes! That graceful, long neck."

Taylor clutched her neck.

"But the reason that I am sure — certain beyond doubt — you were once Nefertiti is in your bag."

"My bag?" Taylor grabbed the daypack she'd tossed on the chair beside her.

"Look inside," Dr. Bey said.

Nervously, Taylor fumbled with the bag's drawstring. She saw what he was talking about right away.

The blue scarab sat in the center of the bag.

Taylor looked at Dr. Bey in alarm. "This wasn't here when I came in. They searched my bag."

"I saw it when you took out your phone," Dr. Bey told her. "That's when I knew."

"Knew what? That I'm a thief?! Because I'm not! I've been trying to get rid of this thing! I even dumped it in the trash at the airport."

"Dumped a priceless treasure in the trash?" Dr. Bey asked, shocked.

"I know how it sounds, but — this scarab has been following me."

"And it always will."

"What do you mean?"

Dr. Bey slowly stood. "There's much to explain. I will come to see you and your parents tomorrow. Tell them to expect me at eight."

"But, Dr. Bey, what —"

Dr. Bey didn't wait for her to finish her question. He bowed to Taylor and then seemed to disappear into the darkness.

Where had he gone?

Taylor grabbed her pack and hurried out of the aisle after him. The light from the stage allowed her to see well enough to make her way up the aisle. She wanted to give him the scarab to hold on to. What if those people from the cab ride came back, or Valdry?

When Taylor got to the end of the aisle, she

stepped into a circle of red light from the exit sign and paused. It felt like someone was staring at her, and Taylor swung around toward an open side door.

The little girl from the hotel stood in the doorway, framed by the bright light from the museum. For a moment, she and Taylor stared at each other. This was definitely a child — no old woman.

"Taylor!" Mrs. Mason called from the stage, searching for Taylor. "Where are you?"

"Up here!" Taylor shouted back.

Turning toward the little girl again, Taylor found that the door was shut and the girl was gone.

THAT EVENING Taylor sat on the small balcony outside her hotel room with Jason beside her. Even from the third floor, the sound of traffic below still rumbled. A warm breeze ruffled her hair as she cradled the blue scarab in her cupped hands. It was quiet — no humming or movement — as though it were asleep.

"How did your parents react when you told

them what Dr. Bey said?" Jason asked. He'd been out all day on the Nile with his mother and some of the others from the trip. Ribbons of sunburn striped his forehead, cheeks, and chin.

"I didn't — not yet."

"Why not?"

Taylor sighed. "Maybe I want them to hear it from Dr. Bey when he comes over tomorrow night. If I tell them they'll just think I've gone crazy. They'll worry or send me to a doctor or something. I don't want to miss a minute of this trip shut in the hotel room because they think I've got sunstroke or some other problem."

"How did you feel when he said it?" Jason asked. "Do you think it could be true?"

Taylor tilted her chair back onto two legs and balanced with her feet against the balcony wall. How did she feel? It was difficult to explain, but a memory kept coming back to her.

"Once I was in the ancient Egyptian section at the Metropolitan Museum of Art," Taylor recalled. "I stood near the reconstruction of the Temple of Dendur, and I had the strongest feeling that I'd seen something like it in a past life. Then I looked around, and all the people were reading the little plaques and studying the surrounding art. Judging from their intense expressions, I thought, they all seemed to have that reincarnated feeling. But *then* I remembered that the ancient Egyptian empire lasted over two thousand years — that's a lot of people who might have lived a life back then, even more than one lifetime."

"Then you do think it's possible?" Jason said.

"Reincarnation? Sure. It sort of makes sense. But for me to be . . ."

"Could Dr. Bey be right?"

It sounded so crazy. She'd heard of deluded people who believed they were Napoleon or Joan of Arc. Wasn't this just the same? "I don't know," Taylor said.

"Would you like it if it turned out to be true?"

"Not if this creepy scarab keeps following me around and setting off airport security alarms," Taylor said, smiling.

"No, seriously — don't you think it would be cool?"

"It makes me worry," Taylor replied sincerely. "It's so much responsibility. If I'm an ancient princess, what am I expected to do? It scares me. Right now I just want to be a regular girl — a tourist — seeing Egypt with her parents."

Taylor turned the scarab over in her hands, and then stood up. "I've got to find some place to put this."

"Each room has a small safe with a key. It's in the front closet," Jason said.

With a nod, Taylor left the balcony and headed for the closet. After depositing the scarab inside, she locked the safe carefully and tucked the key inside a zippered pocket in her daybag.

"It should be safe there," Jason said.

"I only hope it *stays* there," Taylor said.

· · ·

The next day Taylor sat beside Jason and gazed out the window at the Nile River on her left. They were riding an air-conditioned minibus carrying her parents, Jason, his mother, and four more members of their university tour group.

In the front seat, their guide, Professor Johnson — a stout man with glasses wearing a safari-style helmet — spoke about Amarna, which had once been called Akhetaten, the seat of Pharaoh Akhenaten's kingdom.

"'Something's rotten in Akhetaten,' said Akhenaten," Jason joked in a whisper.

Taylor smiled. "'You're right, sweetie,' said Nefertiti."

There was still another hour to go before they reached Minya, the small town where they would stop for lunch before taking a motorboat the rest of the way to what was left of ancient Amarna.

For the next hour, Jason napped while Taylor pressed her head against the glass, watching the majesty of the Nile River race past. Palm trees lined the shore and the areas near the river were much greener than inland. Many riverboats and sailboats cruised along its vivid blue waters.

Soon her eyes felt heavy and she closed them, lost in a dream.

She wore a long, cone-shaped crown like the kind Nefertiti wore, and a white gown that tied at her waist. She talked to a slim man whose tall crown was also made of gold.

"The nights exhaust me so, my queen," the man said, as the first rays of dawn streamed in through long windows.

"Aten be praised," Taylor said to him. "We are safe for another day, dear Akhenaten."

The Pharaoh Akhenaten held the blue scarab up to the window. "Our greatest treasure," he said. "How would we ever live without it?"

As he held the scarab, it disappeared out of his hand . . .

. . . and appeared in Nefertiti's lap.

"I thought we would be safe by moving all the way out here, away from the old capital at Thebes," Nefertiti said, "But, alas, it seems they have followed us even here."

"Thank the heavens we have you to keep us safe."

"True," Nefertiti said, lifting the scarab, "but for how long?"

"For as long as you rule and keep control of the scarab," Akhenaten said.

"I cannot live and rule forever," Nefertiti said. "When I depart this earth, what will become of our people?"

"There are things we can do, my dearest one — in this lifetime and the lifetimes to come — to protect the people. I will consult my advisers and priests."

"I don't want to live forever," Nefertiti said.

Akhenaten sat beside her. "Unfortunately, that may be our only choice."

15

"TAKE A moment to reapply your sunscreen," Professor Johnson advised the group as they emerged from the bus. "You'll find very little shade here."

The flecked, broken stones at Amarna glittered in the scorching desert sun. There wasn't a lot of the ruined city to see — some broken columns, chipped steps, and slanted, once-rectangular doorways. A tall tower reflected the glistening sunlight. The foundations of the ancient, ruined city were still evident, but the buildings were mostly gone.

"I'm so glad we made this trip," Mrs. Mason said to Taylor as they walked through the ruins. "I can picture it as it must have been — such a magnificent place. I'll be able to add so many details to my play."

"I wish more of it were still here," Taylor said, squinting against the intense light.

"There is more at the Egyptian Museum in Cairo," Professor Mason said. "They have a great exhibit right now with a full re-creation of the city. You didn't get to see it yesterday, but we'll certainly be back there during this trip."

"I wonder what Dr. Bey wants to talk to us about tonight," Mrs. Mason said. "Any ideas?"

"Maybe he'll offer me a job," Professor Mason

replied with a chuckle. "What do you think, Taylor? Want to live in Cairo?"

"I don't know . . ." Taylor said, still pondering her dream. "I doubt he'll offer you a job, anyway."

Professor Mason pouted and seemed offended.

"No offense, Dad," Taylor said. "He only just met you yesterday."

Taylor's parents strolled forward to stay with the group but Taylor lagged behind, trying to imagine the city as it once had been, and as her mom had been able to picture so easily. She'd seen artists' renderings that showed it as a mostly open space with tall pillars and angular buildings. There was something about the place that struck Taylor as being strangely modern. It seemed to her that it had been designed to allow in as much sun as possible.

The dream she'd had on the bus had been so real. And now that she was standing here in Amarna, ancient Akhetaten, it seemed to her that this was exactly where it had taken place.

So had she seen something from the past? How could she have known what the city looked like, what it would feel like to stand inside, if she'd never been there? And why would the scarab be the greatest treasure of the pharaoh and his wife when Professor Johnson had said they had tons of jewels and gold?

The scarab was made of only semiprecious stone. It was just a scarab, in an era when so many of them had been made.

"Water?" Jason offered, coming up beside her and holding out a metal canteen.

"Nice! An old-school canteen," Taylor said, taking a swig.

"I don't believe in bottled water — all that waste."

Taylor nodded and wiped her mouth. "Same. Thanks." Together they caught up with the rest of the group.

Professor Johnson continued his talk, pointing out that the city had been built with cliffs on three sides and close to the Nile River.

He moved on toward a set of stone steps and the group followed, with Taylor hanging back. "Come on," Jason said to her.

"Wait." A dizzy feeling had come over Taylor. She held on to Jason's arm to stay upright. "I need to sit for a minute."

"Should I get your parents?" Jason asked.

Taylor spied them at the front of the crowd, deeply absorbed in Professor Johnson's talk. "No. They'll just make a fuss. I'll be okay in a minute."

Jason walked her over to a patch of shade in a corner where two broken walls butted each other. "Have some more water," he said, offering his canteen again.

Leaning against the broken wall, Taylor took a sip, and the dizziness left her. "Thanks, that really helps. Go hear the talk. I'm just going to stay here a minute more to rest. Then I'll join you."

"Okay. Are you sure you're all right? You were sick just before we came to Egypt. Maybe you're not all better."

"I'm fine, it's just all the sun. I need some shade."

Jason headed toward the group. Watching him, Taylor stood and took in the scene around her. In the sky, the sun blazed. Taylor once more pictured the scene from her dream where Akhenaten held the scarab up to the window and claimed it was his greatest treasure.

A buzzing sensation began in Taylor's fingertips and grew stronger. Disturbed, Taylor put Jason's canteen on the wall so she could shake her hand to get the blood flowing again. Why was her hand suddenly going numb?

The numbness was becoming painful. Taylor rubbed both palms together but that didn't make it any better.

It was as though hundreds of insects were pinching her.

Taylor clenched her hand into a fist and then unclenched it, repeating the motion over and over. It seemed to help the pain but her hand was becoming hot — and then she saw it!

The blue scarab appeared in her right hand.

This was insane! How had the scarab gotten out of the safe?

Taylor trembled — she had to find her parents.

As she turned to go, the sand in front of her swirled. Taylor stepped away from it but the size of the vortex only grew wider, its circumference expanding by the second.

As she stared at the spinning sand, amazed and terrified — a man's hand arose from the center.

It clasped an iron grip around Taylor's ankle, and with one powerful yank pulled her down under the sand.

16

WE HAVE it! Ha!"

Taylor lay flat on a cool floor. The man kneeling at her side had snatched the scarab from her palm just as her eyes fluttered open. She wiped the sand from her face and coughed, pulling herself to sitting.

She was in a high-ceilinged room of polished, golden stone. Several torches threw light against the shimmering walls and across the floor of patterned tile.

In one corner, a monstrous statue of a winged bat with fanged teeth and red eyes appeared poised to lunge at them. A ring of short torches lit him from below, throwing terrifying shadows over his face.

In the shifting amber light, Taylor recognized the man at her side.

"Valdry!" Taylor cried, and coughed again. "How did I get here?"

Valdry nodded toward a winding slide in the corner of the room.

A young woman stepped out from behind the slide, the one with the painted-on eyebrows whom Taylor had given the scarab to that day she rode with Sharon to the Haunted Museum. Beside her was the little girl Taylor had encountered in the hotel lobby and later in the theater.

But they looked strikingly different. All three of them had eyes completely lacking in color. Their white irises swam in the white field of their eyes. The eerie effect was that the black of their pupils were like ebony holes that bored into her.

"I gave you the scarab," Taylor spoke to the young woman from the Haunted Museum.

The young woman's face contorted with anger and her pupils suddenly flashed a red beam of light, just like the red flashes Taylor had seen coming from behind her sunglasses.

"You gave it to me, but you stole it back!" the woman said.

"I didn't!"

"Then how did you get it again?" The red beam from the woman's eyes bored into the side of Taylor's neck. It burned, and Taylor clapped her hand over it.

"I don't know." The vein in Taylor's neck pounded hard against her fingers.

The woman shot another fierce look at Taylor and her eyes emitted more rays. Taylor withstood it for as long as she could but finally had to let go. She turned her back on the woman, feeling the burn shift to the back of her neck. "Stop that!" Taylor said. "It hurts!"

"We can do a lot worse than that to you," the woman threatened.

"Stop, Sethor," the child spoke up forcefully.

Instantly the heat on Taylor's neck faded. Taylor turned toward Sethor. Her eyes were once again white.

"Thank you," Taylor said to the child. "You have the scarab now. I only want to get out of here."

As she spoke, Taylor rubbed her burning hand.

It was tingling, and she assumed it was the pain left from the red burn. But suddenly, the scarab popped into her palm.

"How are you doing that?!" Valdry shouted.

"I don't know!" Taylor cried, but Valdry began to cast a furious red beam in Taylor's direction. This time it was aimed directly at her heart.

Taylor leaped out of the beam's path, but Valdry followed her motions, glowering hatefully.

"Valdry, cease!" the little girl cried out.

"Yes, Simone," Valdry said, bowing.

Taylor studied the child and realized that once again she had transformed into a wrinkled and stooped old woman.

"How can she tell us of her powers when the two of you are burning holes in her?"

Valdry and Sethor mumbled apologies.

"There will be time for that later," Simone added quietly.

Taylor heard Simone's comment and began scanning the room for exits. What was she planning to do *later*?

Simone held Taylor's hand in her own claw-like, icy-cold grasp, which, despite its tiny size, was surprisingly strong. "The scarab reacts like that for one person only — Nefertiti!"

"But she's just a child," Sethor said.

"Foolish girl!" Simone scolded Sethor. "Nefertiti has incarnated many times. Each time she has devoted herself to destroying us, and each time we have destroyed her. But she is back again and has uncovered the power of the scarab once more."

"This girl?!" Valdry challenged Simone. "Impossible!"

"Very possible and very true!" Simone shouted

at Valdry. "This girl must be destroyed before she destroys us!"

As they argued, Taylor's heart pounded. She wasn't sure how she could be a threat to these creatures, but one thing was certain — she couldn't give them the chance to *destroy* her.

17

TAYLOR DECIDED that her only hope was a six-foot rectangle cut into the side of the wall across from her. There was no handle on it, but at least it was shaped like a door. It would be the first place she'd try if she saw her chance.

"I have no powers," Taylor said. "It's the scarab's power. It keeps coming back to me on its own. I can't control it."

"Nefertiti couldn't control the scarab at first. She learned quickly, though," Simone said. "Clearly you are Nefertiti reborn again, and you will also learn."

"Who are you? How do you know all this?" Taylor asked.

"Have you ever heard of the Vampya?" Simone asked.

"You're vampires?!" Taylor cried.

Her three captors all smiled at once.

"Do you see fangs?" Sethor asked.

Taylor shook her head.

"That's because we have none," Simone said. "Vampires came later and are much less powerful. Vampya would never bite flesh. That's so crude. We use the power of our eyes to bore into veins until the blood spills."

Taylor tried to appear strong, not to flinch at

the gory image. "How often do you kill?" she asked.

Simone shrugged as if the question was of little importance. "It depends on how much blood we need. Twice a year we drain an entire human and offer the blood to our god, Nezzamort, the sworn enemy of Aten." She gestured at the grotesque statue in the corner.

"He's the enemy of the sun?" Taylor questioned.

Valdry stepped closer. "We are *all* sworn enemies of the sun. We have to offer him a sacrifice soon, and what better than the blood of Nefertiti?"

"I'm not Nefertiti," Taylor said, backing away from them in the direction of the rectangular cutout.

"Give us that scarab," Simone demanded.

Taylor remembered one of her visions and glanced at the light flickering on the walls.

"Take it!" she said, throwing the scarab toward one of the flaming torches. The moment the scarab hit the fire, a white flash blossomed all around them, illuminating the room with a blinding light.

Simone, Sethor, and Valdry screamed, but Taylor couldn't see them because the light was so bright. Shielding her eyes, she stumbled toward the rectangle.

Taylor reached the rectangle and felt for the cut in the stone. When she found it, she pushed hard, and the stone moved. Pushing again, the stone gave way.

Taylor stepped out the other end — into nothing but air. Flailing her arms and kicking, she tried to grasp something as she fell deeper into the black tunnel of nothingness. She screamed until abruptly she couldn't make a sound.

Water poured into her open mouth, choking off her breath. In the blackness surrounding her, she couldn't see anything at all, but knew she was in liquid, probably underwater — quickly rushing water.

Pumping her arms and legs desperately, Taylor pushed upward with all her strength until she came above the surface, gasping and coughing. No sooner had she swallowed her first gulp of air when she was slapped in the face with a small wave.

Taylor sputtered, her arms flailing, as the strong current carried her along, scraping her against rocks hard enough to bruise. Tossed by the forceful flow, Taylor flipped and spun in the torrent. She had only one thought: to keep her head up and to avoid swallowing the water crashing around her. Was there an end to this powerful current?

Water slapped Taylor in the face again, knocking her below the surface. As she struggled upward, Taylor became aware of a change.

The water had become warmer, and much less turbulent.

With a strong kick, Taylor propelled herself up and came above the surface. The water was calm now, and glinted in the bright sunshine. Hot air seared her throat as she breathed in deeply. Palm trees lined the nearby banks, and out in the middle of the water, Taylor saw the ferry that had brought her tour group to Amarna. It was headed toward the dock where they'd landed earlier, which was just a few yards away on the shore.

She was in the Nile River!

Taylor swam hard toward the water's edge, and it wasn't long before she staggered up onto the banks of the Nile. As she dropped to sit in the smooth silt mud, she felt her cell phone in her back pocket and pulled it out. Completely dead!

There was no way to contact anyone.

What if Sethor, Valdry, and Simone came after her? Suddenly frightened once more, Taylor stood and turned in a circle, searching for them.

Suddenly a voice called out. "There she is!"

Taylor was about to dive back into the Nile on instinct when she saw Jason run out onto the dock. Her parents were right behind him.

Taylor stumbled toward them as they raced in her direction. When they met, Mrs. Mason wrapped Taylor in a panicked hug. Professor Mason enfolded them both but then pulled back. "What happened to you?" he asked.

"Were you in the water?" Mrs. Mason asked.

Taylor opened her mouth to speak but hesitated. How could she explain this? Would they believe her — would anyone?

Straight to bed with you," Mrs. Mason said to Taylor when they got into their hotel room late that afternoon. "I want you to rest."

"I'm fine," Taylor said.

"No, you're not. That sun was simply too strong for you," Professor Mason said as he headed into his bedroom.

"He's right," said Mrs. Mason.

Taylor looked at her mother, disappointed that her parents doubted that what happened to her had been real. Like everyone but Jason, Mrs. Mason thought Taylor had simply wandered off with a bad case of sunstroke.

"I want you to take a nap before Dr. Bey gets here," Mrs. Mason said. "I'm going to take a nap, too."

"Can I take a shower?"

"All right but don't be long. And take your room key."

With a towel, toiletry bag, and change of clothing in a tote bag, Taylor walked down the quiet, dimly lit hallway to the shared bathroom at the end of the hall. She was happy to find it empty and used her room key to unlock it.

Taylor latched the door for added security and turned on the water. A shower would feel wonderful. She was about to undress when she noticed that a black splotch had appeared in the center of the window. It was about the size of her two hands spread wide. It was followed by another black shape of about the same size. Then another . . . and another. In a few moments, the light from outside had been completely blocked out by the splotches, and Taylor stood in total darkness.

What was happening?

Groping in the dark, she searched the wall for a light switch, but couldn't find one. She found the doorknob and pulled on it — the door wouldn't budge. Then she recalled that she'd latched it. Feeling along the door, she located the latch. She expected it to move smoothly out of the locked position, but it seemed stuck.

It would help if she could see!

Feeling her way along the wall, she bumped into the toilet bowl and closed the lid, then climbed on top of it. The window was right above it, and to her relief she discovered it wasn't locked but easily pulled inward.

At first she was happy that it was still light out. In the next second, though, she saw what was covering the window. Black bats were stuck to the glass somehow, their large wings overlapping one another.

Stirred by the movement of the glass, the first bat flew up, flapping its wings into Taylor's face. Startled and terrified, Taylor fell backward off the toilet onto the floor.

In the light let in by the open window, she could see more and more bats flying into the bathroom. They let out shrill squeaks as they swooped around the room, their eyes glowing red.

A bat dove toward Taylor's head.

Shrieking, she swatted at it.

Two more bats attacked her, their small, shiny

claws yanking at her hair. The bats massed around her, spinning in a circle, whirling faster and faster.

With her hands over her head, Taylor tried to fend off the bats, but they just kept swirling in an ever-tightening circle around her. Their squealing filled the room. Taylor wanted to cover her ears but she needed her arms to protect herself.

It was more than she could stand! In another moment she would surely faint — but she couldn't let that happen. What would they do to her if she collapsed? Swatting at the bats once more, Taylor slipped on a rug and fell. There was a second of pain as her head struck the hard counter — and then all she saw was black.

19

TAYLOR RAISED her head and looked around. The last, gray light of day that once more shone through the window told her that she was still in the bathroom, on the tile floor. The right temple of her forehead throbbed with pain.

But the bats were gone.

A line of vivid blue light snapped over her head. It hit the steamy shower door, forming a hair-thin mark of cracked glass. On the other side, the shower continued to run.

Sitting up, Taylor searched for the source of the blue light.

The scarab sat on the floor beside her.

Taylor wasn't even surprised to discover that it was back. By now she was getting used to its strange ability to keep returning.

The scarab zapped the shower door with another shot of blue light. This time Taylor heard a *clink*, and moisture formed on the outside of the chipped glass.

Taylor stared at the scarab. It wanted to get into the shower.

Lifting the scarab and cupping it in her palm, she once again felt the tingle of electricity run from her hand and up her arm. Her heart beat faster as she pulled the door open and peered into the stall. Immediately she saw the black bat clinging to the wall behind the shower faucet's spray.

Before Taylor could react, the scarab hit the bat with its laser. The creature squealed as it slid down the wall into the tub, its blood swirling around the drain.

The scarab had saved her from the bats. It was the only answer that made sense. Looking away from the bat, Taylor reached up to shut the shower.

A hard knock sounded on the bathroom door. "Are you all right in there, Taylor?" Mrs. Mason called. "You've been in there a long time."

Taylor set down the scarab on the sink and went to the door.

"You're not even showered," her mother noticed when Taylor opened the door. "What happened?"

Taylor gazed at her mother, not sure how to respond. Was she going to tell her another wild story of how she'd been attacked by bats and the scarab had saved her?

"I slipped and hit my head," Taylor said. This was at least part of the truth.

"Oh no!" Mrs. Mason cried. "After all you've been through today!" She stepped into the steamy bathroom. "Are you all right? How do you feel?"

"My head hurts," Taylor said. "I'm okay otherwise."

"Did you hit your head on the shower glass? It's cracked."

"I — there's a dead bat in the shower," Taylor warned her mother as Mrs. Mason went to examine the cracked shower stall.

Mrs. Mason's hands flew to her heart in alarm. "Oh! And it scared you! You poor thing! This hotel is the worst. First bugs, now this."

The hotel wasn't fancy but it was clean and

neat. "It's not the hotel, Mom. Something strange is going on."

Mrs. Mason opened her mouth to reply but then let out a sudden yelp of surprise and jumped back. She'd noticed the blue scarab sitting in the sink. "How did that get there?"

"I don't know, Mom. It just keeps coming back to me. That's part of what I'm trying to tell you."

A thousand thoughts seemed to flash across Mrs. Mason's face as she attempted to make sense of what Taylor had just said. "I know what's happening," she said finally. "I went online and searched the Haunted Museum. At first I didn't find much, but then I began reading the comments some of the people had left on the museum's website."

"What did they say?" Taylor asked.

"Some people reported that after they had

touched one of the items in the museum, strange things began happening to them."

"Strange things like what?"

"The item that the person had touched seemed to come back to haunt him or her. Some of the stories were extremely frightening."

"Are you saying that the scarab comes back to me all the time because I touched it?" Taylor asked.

"It must be," Mrs. Mason replied.

"Actually, that's only part of the story," said someone out in the hallway. Taylor and her mother turned to see Dr. Bey standing in the open bathroom doorway. "In this case, the story is much more complex than that."

20

Back in the Masons' hotel room, Dr. Bey sat in a chair and laid five golden tiles out on the desk in front of him. Taylor and her parents sat in chairs on the other side of the desk and gazed down at the images etched into the gold. They were done in the same odd style as the other art from the Amarna period.

In all the tiles, lines of sunlight shone down on different scenes. Mostly the tiles seemed to show

Pharaoh Akhenaten and Queen Nefertiti enjoying the sunlight along with their children. The fifth tile was slightly different. In it, Nefertiti held the sun and its rays shone out in front of her.

"I don't believe it," Taylor murmured as she studied the tile.

Nefertiti was shining the light of the sun on a bat.

Dr. Bey nodded. "You see these etchings differently now, don't you?"

Taylor looked up into his eyes. Could it be true? It suddenly all seemed so obvious. "Everyone thinks that's the sun in these tiles but it's not, is it?"

"Smart young lady," he said, pointing to the large, blue scarab sitting on the desk. "No, it's this. This scarab is the thing that they're showing. The rays are the blue beams that protected the people from the Vampya."

"The Vampya!" Mrs. Mason said with a gasp.

"Are you sure?" Professor Mason asked skeptically. "All the scholars who study this period are convinced that Akhenaten and Nefertiti worshipped the sun — not a scarab."

"They worshipped both," Dr. Bey replied. "The light of the sun kept them safe from the Vampya, for whom sunlight is dangerous. That's why when the Vampya grew powerful and became a threat, Akhenaten moved his kingdom and built a palace in the sunniest place he could find. Akhetaten was built so that very few shady places existed in the city streets. But every night, the sun set, and the people were once more vulnerable to attack from the Vampya. Many were killed — drained of all their blood — during the night."

"And the scarab fought off the Vampya by night," Taylor said, somehow knowing this was true.

"Yes," Dr. Bey said. "Once they found the scarab, the people could protect themselves without the light of day."

"Found?" Professor Mason asked.

"Nefertiti was walking in the desert one day when she stepped into a cave to get out of the sun. There she found a small girl who seemed lost and afraid. When Nefertiti went to help the child, red beams shot out of her eyes, and Nefertiti's wrists began to bleed."

"I met that child," Taylor said with a shudder, remembering Simone.

"Just when Nefertiti felt she would faint, a blue light knocked the girl down. Screaming, the girl ran out into the desert. A second blue light restored Nefertiti to health. The scarab had saved the queen of the Egyptian people."

"Wait a minute," Professor Mason said. "Where did the magical scarab come from?"

"No one knows for certain," Dr. Bey said. He turned over the last tile, the one that showed Nefertiti using the scarab to battle the Vampya. "The people were safe as long as Nefertiti had control of the scarab," Dr. Bey continued. "But, in a way, the scarab turned out to be a curse for the queen."

"In what way?" Taylor asked.

"The only way that the Vampya could be destroyed forever was to put an end to their leader, Nezzamort."

"I saw a statue of him," Taylor said. "Is he real?"

"The legends say he was a real creature," Dr. Bey replied. "The reason Nefertiti disguised herself as Smenkhkare was so she could keep on fighting Nezzamort and the Vampya and keep her people safe even after Akhenaten died."

"She didn't succeed in the end, though, did

she?" Taylor asked. "If she had, the Vampya wouldn't still be around."

"No." Dr. Bey looked out the window at the full moon. "When the Vampya manage to get possession of the scarab, they can only hold on to it until the next full moon. On the full moon the scarab always returns to Nefertiti in any of her forms. But if they can kill Nefertiti before the moon is full, they will be rid of her until her next incarnation. Nefertiti has incarnated again and again, trying to kill Nezzamort with the blue scarab, but each time she fails and is killed instead."

Taylor didn't like the sound of this. If she was Nefertiti, would she also be forced to destroy Nezzamort? And would she be killed trying?

"I'm sorry, Dr. Bey, but this is all just too hard to believe," Professor Mason said, standing. "If this Nezzamort comes near Taylor, I'm simply going to call the police." He took the scarab off the desk and handed it to Dr. Bey. "Please, take this as our contribution to the museum's collection."

Dr. Bey put it back on the desk. "I can't accept it. This belongs to Taylor. It will keep returning to her no matter what I do. And she needs it for protection."

· · ·

Later that evening Jason came by the hotel room. Her parents locked the scarab in the hotel room safe again and went downstairs to socialize with the other adult members of the trip. They left strict orders for Taylor to call them the moment Jason left. They didn't want her staying in the room alone.

Taylor sat cross-legged on the couch and

thumbed through a large book of Egyptian art while Jason sprawled on the floor searching the Internet on his tablet. "Wow! Look at this," he said moving on up to the couch to show Taylor the screen. "The person on this website claims that Nefertiti has reincarnated as Cleopatra, Marie Antoinette, Isadora Duncan, and Marilyn Monroe."

"That's some list," Taylor said. "A queen, a queen, a famous dancer, and a movie star." She studied the dates of their births and deaths. "All these women died before they were old. Cleopatra killed herself with a poisonous snake, Marie Antoinette was beheaded, Isadora Duncan accidentally strangled herself with her own scarf, and Marilyn Monroe killed herself."

"Could the Vampya really have gotten all of them?" Jason asked. "Maybe they just made the deaths look like suicides and accidents."

"I don't know if I believe all that," Taylor said, but a wave of cold fear swept through her anyway. She was so much younger than all these women had been when they died. But would her fate be the same in the end — a victim of the Vampya?

21

Around eleven, Taylor's parents returned and Jason headed back to his own room. "I'm going to be up all night to see if I can find anything else," he said at the door. "So call me if you can't sleep."

"Why — so you can give me more creepy info?" Taylor said lightly.

"What creepy info?" Mrs. Mason asked as Jason left.

"Oh, nothing — just Vampya stuff he saw on the Internet."

"We spoke to people about the Vampya, and most of them said it's just a legend," Professor Mason told Taylor. "It's nothing to take seriously."

"What about this afternoon in Amarna, or what just happened to me in the bathroom?" Taylor asked. What would it take to convince them? "I saw the scarab work with my own eyes."

"She's right. How can we explain that?" Mrs. Mason asked.

Professor Mason opened the room safe and took out the scarab. He placed it on the table. "There's nothing cursed or haunted about this scarab. It's going back to the Egyptian Museum in Cairo where it belongs, first thing in the morning."

"But I saw it work," Taylor said.

"Let's be logical, Taylor," Professor Mason said. "Bats roost in the eaves of this hotel. You startled them when you opened the window. They flew in and in a panic, you slipped or fainted. While you were out cold, you dreamed that the scarab saved you but actually, the bats simply flew back out the window. When Mom knocked, you woke up."

"Thanks for the trust, Dad," Taylor said.

"I trust you. I just think you're confused."

"What about those people who surrounded the cab?"

"What? Are you telling me they were vampires?" Professor Mason asked.

"Not vampires — the Vampya!"

"It's pretty much the same thing, don't you think?" her father said.

Taylor huffed angrily. There was no sense arguing with him. He simply refused to believe it.

"Let's get some sleep," Mrs. Mason said. "I have to be back at the museum for another rehearsal tomorrow morning."

"And I want to join the tour group headed for the pyramids. Are you coming along, Taylor?"

"Sure. I wouldn't miss that."

Her cell phone buzzed, and Taylor took it from the desk where she'd left it. It was a text from Jason about the next day's pyramid trip. He wanted to know if she was going and she texted back that she was.

"Get to bed," Mrs. Mason called from her room.

Putting her phone back on the desk beside the scarab, Taylor went to her room and quickly fell into a deep sleep.

Taylor dreamed she was walking in a vast desert with nothing nearby but sand dunes. Her sandal hit a hard object and she knelt to see what it was. A large blue scarab sat in the sand.

"Khepri," she said, picking up the scarab. Somehow she knew it meant "He who came forth from the earth" and seemed like a fitting name. Cupping the scarab in her hands, she bent and kissed it.

When Taylor woke up two hours later, she had the feeling that some noise had caused her to awaken.

There it was! A scratch as though someone in the outside room had knocked into a chair.

She heard it again. Somebody was definitely out there. It wasn't one of her parents, either. They'd have turned on a lamp, and no light shone under the door.

Too scared to turn on her own lamp, Taylor searched in the moonlight for her phone so she could call her parents in their room. Where was it? Had she brought it in with her?

No! It was still on the desk!

Taylor heard the sound of the sliding glass door onto the balcony being opened and then closed. If the thief was outside, maybe she could make it over to her phone and then crawl back to her room.

Cracking open her door, Taylor peered out. Moonlight gave the room a soft glow, and right away Taylor noticed that her phone was on the desk — and the scarab was no longer there. Turning, she checked her room to see if it had come to her, but didn't see it. No, the scarab was gone.

The room was empty so Taylor felt brave enough to crawl toward her phone. It was possible that the thief had come in and left from the balcony. In that case there was nothing to fear, but just to be safe, she stayed on all fours.

Keeping low, she made her way toward the desk. From the middle of the room, she had a good view of the balcony. No one was out there so Taylor stood up, only to find that the blue scarab was now perched on the railing of the balcony.

Why had the thief left it there?

Taylor's heartbeat quickened as she slid back the door to the balcony. She didn't want the scarab to fall to the sidewalk below.

As soon as Taylor wrapped her hand around the scarab, a shadow fell over her.

An unpleasant musky smell filled the air and Taylor was aware of the warmth of another presence.

Slowly she lifted her eyes.

Perched on the balcony railing was a creature nearly ten feet high.

It was Nezzamort — half-man, half-bat.

Before Taylor could move, the beast clutched her under her right armpit, its talons digging in painfully, and grabbed the scarab with its other claw.

Screaming, Taylor was lifted into the air, her legs and arms flailing, as Nezzamort carried her off into the night.

22

Taylor DARED to open her eyes. The bright, colorful lights of Cairo twinkled below her. Instantly she squeezed her eyes shut once more. They were flying so high up!

What if Nezzamort dropped her?!

Taylor clutched on to the creature's rough leg just in case he decided to let go. A warm breeze swept her hair back and made her clothing flutter. Under other circumstances she might have been thrilled at this open-air journey, but at the moment she was too terrified to enjoy the experience.

After another few minutes, she summoned the courage for a second peek. The colors of Cairo had receded and now sand dunes lay gorgeous and silent below them.

After almost twenty minutes, Nezzamort spread his wings wide and descended into the center of the city that had once been Akhetaten. The ruins shimmered in the moonlight. The beast gently deposited the scarab on a stone slab, but kept his talon on Taylor, who remained in his grip and lay flat in the sand.

An old woman this time, Simone stepped out from behind a slab of rock, her wiry white hair creating a halo effect around her haggard face, and her colorless eyes seeming to glow. She bowed low to Nezzamort. "O, great one, you have triumphed," she said.

Valdry and Sethor joined Simone. "At last," Valdry said, staring down at Taylor with his white eyes, "this is the moment we have waited centuries for."

"Nefertiti and her power over the scarab will finally be ended," Simone went on. "We will sacrifice you to Nezzamort tonight, on the full moon. Your soul will be trapped with Nezzamort, no longer able to travel and fight the Vampya forever. The scarab will remain under our power, and then nothing can stop the rise of the Vampya. The world will be ours!"

Nezzamort lifted his talon from Taylor and she inhaled, once more able to breathe freely without his crushing weight on her. Standing, she looked around frantically. Her mind raced, trying to form a plan.

The only place to run would be the police booth down by the Nile. She could outrun Simone for sure, and probably Sethor and Valdry.

Then she thought of Nezzamort. There would be no escaping him.

But Nezzamort had already lifted off into the sky, his wings outlined in the full moon. He perched on a tall stone rectangle that had once been a doorway and settled there, folding his immense wings around himself.

Taylor dug her bare heels into the sand, preparing to spring forward to escape. Before she could move, though, she sensed movement around her.

The ragged people who had surrounded the cab were moving in a slow, steady pace, forming a knot around Taylor and her three captors. Their expressionless faces made Taylor think of zombies, but their ripped clothing reminded her of mummies. Either way, her heart sank.

The strange people came from all directions. Simone, Sethor, and Valdry stepped away to allow the creatures to tighten their knot around Taylor.

As they closed in, she saw they wore the same bat amulets as they had the other day at the cab. They stank of unwashed and rotted flesh. Taylor had never experienced such an awful stench.

"Come, my helpers," Simone commanded them. "This is the moment that you servants of the Vampya have been working toward for so long."

The servants of the Vampya pressed in closer and closer. Taylor was determined not to faint, but fear and the terrible smell made her stomach clench. Cold beads of sweat formed on her forehead.

A rotted hand with filthy, jagged nails reached out and grabbed a handful of Taylor's hair before yanking her head back painfully. Another one of them poured a vial of steaming liquid down her throat.

Taylor's world spun — and then all she knew was nothingness.

. . .

The next time Taylor opened her eyes, she was in the same open square of the former Akhetaten, but the huge moon that hung in the sky was completely full, lighting everything with a brilliance that made it easy to see.

Taylor quickly realized she was tied to a stone pillar. In front of her stood about fifty people dressed in black with the same pale skin, white eyes, and black hair as Valdry, Sethor, and Simone. The Vampya — it seemed — had all come out for the occasion. Behind them the tattered, dazed servants who had taken her prisoner all stood, shuffling slightly.

As panic set in, Taylor strained against the ropes that held her, and when she moved, bracelets jangled on her arms and legs. Looking down she saw that she wore golden sandals and was dressed in a silk gown of purple and gold. A heavy crown sat on her head.

They'd dressed her as Nefertiti!

At her feet was a large bowl. Its outside was covered in jade and rubies. What were they going to do with it?

A *thwap thwap thwap* of wings caused Taylor to look up.

Nezzamort flew down to settle on top of a high stone doorframe that stood on its own about ten yards away, an ancient monster on an ancient ruin.

Simone, Valdry, and Sethor stepped forward from the crowd of Vampya and approached Taylor. All three of them wore black robes that trailed behind them.

Picking up the bowl, Simone turned to face

Nezzamort and lifted the bowl above her head. "Now, O Nezzamort, will your great enemy be destroyed."

Valdry reached into his robe and took out a cage containing the blue scarab. He opened it, and the scarab did something Taylor never knew it could. With rapidly beating wings and a high-pitched buzz, the scarab burst from the cage and flew to her shoulder, where it perched. It was no longer made of stone, but a living beetle. Its antennae twitched and its tiny black eyes moved back and forth alertly. The scarab's wings were many shades of clear, translucent blue.

"Your secret weapon can't help you now, Nefertiti," Simone shouted. "It comes alive on the full moon so it can fly to you. But that also gives us the chance to kill it. Never before have the Vampya had this opportunity: We have both

Nefertiti and her scarab in our power. There is nothing you can do to stop us!"

Simone turned back to Taylor, and her white eyes — and those of Valdry and Sethor — now shone with red light. Together the threesome approached Taylor.

23

THE BEETLE on Taylor's shoulder buzzed, and its wings fluttered, but it looked as helpless as Taylor felt. And maybe it was as terrified, too.

Would her blood really be drained and sacrificed to Nezzamort? Was that awful beast really going to capture her spirit for all eternity?

Could she allow the people of the earth to fall prey to the Vampya?

Shutting her eyes, she saw a vision of herself as Nefertiti in the desert, picking up the scarab. It was as though wisdom, knowledge, and experience gathered over centuries suddenly swept through her, and a new sense of queenly power filled Taylor.

She wasn't going to let this evil come to the world.

"Khepri, son of Aten, rise once more." Taylor spoke the words, but it hardly seemed that they were coming from her mouth. This voice was speaking through her. "Rise once more, Khepri! I summon you!"

The blue scarab flew from her shoulder and hovered in the air.

Simone stepped back, and her eyes lost their red glow.

Valdry grabbed at the scarab, but each time the blue beetle darted out of his reach.

The scarab rose in the sky, moving higher and higher and growing ever larger. Blue light began to whirl at its underbelly.

Valdry, Sethor, and Simone joined the other Vampya, who were running to escape.

A wide blue light from the gigantic scarab swept across the ground catching all the Vampya in its beam. One by one each of the Vampya exploded until the sky seemed alive with fireworks.

When the last Vampya had exploded, the beam disappeared.

Taylor had a moment of relief, but then noticed that Nezzamort was still on his perching spot, watching.

In a flash he was beside her and seemed three times as large as he had earlier. Ripping the cords that tied her to the stone pillar, Nezzamort lifted her by the arm once more and flew toward the enormous scarab.

The scarab hummed but didn't attack. It was as if it was aware that Nezzamort held Taylor — as though it was considering its next move.

Red beams shot from Nezzamort's eyes and a part of the scarab's wing was blasted away. The beetle dipped but recovered its balance.

Nezzamort shot another beam, and the giant scarab was flung backward, falling just yards from the ground before returning.

Taylor knew the scarab was afraid to hurt her — but it needed to do something, or Nezzamort would kill it!

The scarab flew below the monster and Taylor twisted, watching it. Had the scarab given up? What could she do to help?

Taylor turned to Nezzamort's claw, which was wrapped around her arm, and sunk her teeth deep into it. Roaring with anger, Nezzamort released her, and she tumbled toward the ground.

The scarab rose to catch her fall. Taylor hit the top of its hard shell and then almost rolled off before gripping the edge and pulling herself back on. Lying flat, she held tight while the beetle rose again, swerving to avoid another ray from Nezzamort, then turned to blast the beast.

The blue beam found its target with a spectacular and immense impact. Like the grand finale of a fireworks display, Nezzamort filled the sky with particles of colored light.

Shielding her eyes, Taylor finally looked away, unable to withstand the blinding light and heat from the explosion.

The scarab descended slowly from the sky with Taylor on its back. It grew smaller and smaller as it neared the ground, until it could no longer carry Taylor. Jumping to the sand below, she became aware of a high-pitched siren, and

suddenly the ancient site was awash in red blink-
ing light.

A police van drove into the center of the ruins.
"What's going on here?" a police officer shouted
angrily as he got out of the car, waving his flash-
light. "You people have no permit for fireworks.
And you don't have permission to have a costume
party on this site, either. If you did, I'd have been
notified."

A costume party? Was he kidding?

Then Taylor saw what he meant. Not only was
she dressed as Queen Nefertiti, but there were
people around her dressed in costumes from many
periods of time. Some were dressed as ancient
Egyptians, but others wore hoop skirts or top
hats, and long frock coats. One woman wore a
miniskirt and tall beehive-style hairdo from
the 1960s. Another had on a soldier's uniform

from the First World War. But where had they come from?

While the police officer shone his light on the costumed people, Taylor approached them, studying each face. There were just about as many of them as there had been the torn and tattered servants of the Vampya.

The people themselves seemed confused. "How did I get here?" a woman dressed as a flapper asked Taylor.

"I don't know," Taylor replied honestly.

"The last thing I remember is a man approaching me. And a red light was shooting from his eyes," she added, rubbing her head.

That was it! These were the victims of the Vampya. They had been working secretly in the world for centuries, bringing the people they'd attacked back here to this center in Egypt to be their slaves. Now their victims were free.

That had to mean that the Vampya had truly been destroyed!

"Okay, everybody, the party's over," the officer shouted. "A police ferry will bring you back to Cairo tonight. All of you, clear out! You're lucky I don't arrest you."

Taylor looked down at the blue beetle scuttling through the sand. She watched it burrow down and disappear. Was it just another beetle now that its work was done, or would it forever be Khepri, the mighty slayer of the Vampya?

DAWN'S LIGHT lent everything a bluish cast as Taylor put the key into her hotel room door. Stepping inside, she realized that her parents were still asleep. Good! They hadn't been worried sick all night, or out searching for her.

Walking through the room to the balcony, she picked up her phone, which was still on the hotel desk. Outside, Taylor sat with Nefertiti's long, cone-shaped crown in her lap, thinking about everything that had happened.

Her phone buzzed with a text from Jason. *Taylor? U OK?* Why was he awake? She said she was, and asked what he was doing up.

In a few minutes Jason knocked softly at the door. "Shh," she said, "my parents are still asleep."

"Are you all right? What happened?" Jason asked.

"It's a strange story. I don't know if you'll believe it."

Jason pressed his hand to his forehead and shook his head as if overcome with shock and confusion.

"I saw some *thing* fly away with you," he said. "I was on my balcony late last night on my computer and I saw it. I tried to text you a million times but you didn't answer, so I hoped I'd just fallen asleep and dreamed it."

Taylor checked her phone and smiled at all the messages he'd left.

K?

KK?

Are you all right? Sleeping? Not flying in the sky are you?

They sat down on the balcony side by side. Taylor wasn't sure how much to tell him, but decided that if anyone would believe her, it would be Jason. So she told him exactly what had happened.

". . . so the police let us all go. Can you believe they thought it was a costume party and fireworks?"

"Wow!" Jason said, studying Taylor's face as she finished her story. "I can't believe I know Nefertiti. Are you going to tell the people at the Egyptian Museum in Cairo who you really are?"

"Dr. Bey already knows."

"What about your parents? What will you tell them?"

"The truth. They'll probably think I was dreaming, though."

"Bummer," Jason said.

"Not really. I'll be so glad to get back to normal."

Jason nodded and got up from his chair. "Well, I'm happy you're okay. I couldn't get to sleep until I was sure."

"Thanks. We'd better get some rest before the trip to the pyramids," Taylor said.

"See you later," Jason said.

Walking silently to her room, Taylor stared at

herself in the mirror. She put her crown back on, tucking her hair inside. The black kohl eyeliner the Vampya had rimmed her eyes with had barely smudged in all the commotion.

Taylor turned her head to one side and then to the other, checking her profile with sidelong glances. She did look a lot like Nefertiti.

But was she — really — Nefertiti?

The queen had dedicated her life to protecting her people from the Vampya. She'd even disguised herself as a man — Smenkhkare — so she could continue to fight after the king had died.

Could she go back to being regular old Taylor, now that she had accomplished the thing Nefertiti had dedicated herself to through so many lifetimes? Had she already achieved her life's purpose, before she was even in high school?

No, she decided.

She was far from done.

She was Nefertiti and Taylor both at once. And now that she knew what she was truly capable of — she'd only just begun to do great things.

ABOUT THE AUTHOR

SUZANNE WEYN lives in a valley in New York
State. She's the author of The Haunted Museum
series, The Bar Code series, and the novels *Distant
Waves*, *Dr. Frankenstein's Daughters*, and *Faces
of the Dead* for older readers, and the Breyer
Stablemates books *Diamond* and *Snowflake* for
younger readers.

Amazing
Adventures
You'll Love!